PLANTATION MAN

A NOVEL BY

Hartley Henderson

Melbourne Australia

Hartley Henderson c/- Intertype Publish and Print
Unit 45, 125 Highbury Road
BURWOOD VIC 3125
Australia
www.intertype.com.au

Ordering Information:
Quantity sales. Special discounts are available on quantity purchases by corporations, associations, and others. For details, contact the "Special Sales Department" at the address above.

Plantation Man/ Hartley Henderson. —1st ed.
ISBN 978-0-6453780-1-6

To the memory of my parents John and Ivy, and my sister Marcelle

AUTHOR'S NOTE

For a long time, I have been fascinated by the deep south of America, particularly Louisiana, the city of New Orleans, and life along the Mississippi River. This interest goes way back to my boyhood growing up on a farm and reading over and over Mark Twain's books *The Adventures of Tom Sawyer* and *Adventures of Huckleberry Fin*. In other of his writings, I learnt that Twain (1835 – 1910) was a strong advocate for the abolition of slavery, and that he was also a supporter of women's rights.

Twain's writings provided me not only with an appreciation of the beauty, vibrancy, and color of the deep south, but also an understanding of how brutal life could be on many plantations for black people during the slave-trade period.

Although my *Plantation Man* story commences roughly in the mid-1980s and runs through the 1990s and beyond, the reader will find some references and commentary on the slave-trade era and the importance of continually striving to ensure racial equality. This can be found particularly in the chapter relating to Raoul's funeral in Montgomery.

I have visited the USA many times, including in relation to my work as a freelance writer. On an early trip I traveled across the country on a three-month's Greyhound Bus pass. Although a challenging experience, it proved to be a great way to see the country and meet a wide range of people from various socio-economic backgrounds.

It has been an amazing and exhilarating experience as a writer to 'walk' alongside the main characters presented in this book - Jack, Salina, and   Sam - as I progressed the storyline of the novel, and as various other characters entered and developed. I felt myself becoming almost a participant or companion as the story evolved. In the process, some of my own thoughts about values, views, and attitudes to life surfaced, and sometimes were even slightly modified and reflected in the narrative or dialogue.

Finally, I should emphasize that this book is a work of fiction. Many locations obviously exist, although specific places and events within them may be fictitious. On the other hand, the city of Cranton was wholly invented to suit the storyline. I have attempted, through considerable research, to ensure accuracy to the extent possible in describing real places and I hope that any mistakes are minimal. Even in fictitious places such as Gratton Grange, I have attempted through internet research and my own knowledge of agriculture, to provide a realistic view of the operation of a working plantation in Louisiana.

It is my great hope that readers will enjoy the read as much as I have enjoyed the writing.

CHAPTER 1

The name attached to her apron said Deanna. She handed him a menu and he thanked her by name. She asked what his name was and where he was from.

"Jack Lansell. I'm from New York and tomorrow will start working for a few weeks at the main hospital."

"Welcome to New Orleans. We need all the assistance that we can get right now. Would you like to order?"

"Yes thanks, just a long black coffee and maybe some cake."

"We have a range of cakes including carrot, banana, and of course mud cake, which is our specialty."

"I have noticed that quite a lot of mud remains after the hurricane, so a piece of mud cake would seem appropriate."

Jack observed that two weeks after the hurricane, silt and rubbish still clogged the gutters in the street. He figured this was an indication of the hurricane's strength and the impact of floods which he heard had been caused by broken levees. A gaunt-looking small dog with a limp and no collar rummaged amongst the rubbish.

When she brought his coffee and cake Deanna told him the dog had appeared a few days earlier, that she had named it Lucky, and that it liked cookies. Jack asked her to bring Lucky some cookies and add it to his bill.

A golden rain tree draped with vines dripped moisture onto the sidewalk after a brief summer shower. Across the street honeybees darted in and out of flowers while butterflies laid eggs on the leaves of a magnolia tree which had somehow survived the cyclonic winds.

A tiny lizard scampered down the side of a planter, cocked its head as it looked at him, then darted inside, perhaps seeking a cooler place to rest.

There were very few people passing by. The French Quarter was largely deserted, apart from residents, resilient businesspeople, and the occasional police patrol.

Except from an old lady drinking coffee inside, he was the only customer at the café on a side street. He felt lonely and somewhat out of place, like an interloper in a strange land.

Jack Lansell was 35 and an internationally recognized reconstructive surgeon. He had been invited by Tom Eustace, a surgeon in New Orleans, to assist in dealing with the extensive medical needs following the hurricane. They had become friends when both were studying at med school in Washington DC.

With his medical training, Jack saw himself as being in a privileged position. He felt it was his duty, when the opportunity arose, to assist in improving the lives of those less fortunate. Straight after graduating he went to Africa with the UN to perform reconstructive surgery in several small, impoverished countries. Now, he could not resist the call from Tom to assist in such a challenging situation down south.

Jack's wife Laura had left him the previous year with their eight-year-old son Marcus to live with a well-muscled personal trainer she had met in a local cafe. She was unhappy with the long and irregular hours that Jack worked and the travel that his work sometimes involved. He seemed distant and she felt unloved.

Thinking back over their married life, Jack could not really blame her. He now accepted that he should have established a better balance between work and the responsibilities of his marriage.

Laura had departed with minimal prior discussion. Maybe he should have seen the signs earlier, before recognizing a growing coldness towards him. When she told him she was leaving he tried to discuss the situation with her, but by then it was too late – she had found another man and seemed happy in the new relationship. He was distraught - not only in relation to her decision but also about his own lack of foresight.

During his first couple of weeks in New Orleans he performed numerous operations including realignment of severely fractured and crushed limbs and some limb amputations where gangrene was advanced. He also undertook general surgery in a range of areas where he was not a specialist. Long hours were worked in extremely difficult and challenging conditions with assistance from medical staff who were also exhausted.

One evening after working late, he wandered into a rather down-market bar on the edge of the French Quarter looking for some relaxation with a glass of wine. It provided a chance to reflect on the huge difference between the situation in New Orleans and his home city of New York. The tall buildings reaching to the sky, bright lights and flashy signs, and the crowds of earnest people scurrying here and there on some sort of mission or other. What a contrast, he thought, with the rather desolate scene that confronted him in New Orleans.

There were few customers as he sat at the bar near a tall fit-looking black man of about 40 years of age. After a while the man, who had obviously been there for some time, introduced himself as Sam Gratton. He said he was staying with a friend in an apartment nearby.

The girl behind the bar topped up Sam's glass with cheap white wine but did not look for any payment. His hand shook as he raised the glass and beads of perspiration trickled down the side of his solemn face.

Jack got the impression that this man was just about at the end of his tether and could not take much more of what life was dishing up to him.

"Are you OK?" asked Jack.

"Thanks for your concern. I haven't slept much lately – too much on my mind."

Jack's eyes roamed around the room. It did not look or feel like a friendly place – more like a last-ditch retreat to drown one's sorrows, and perhaps hope for a better day tomorrow.

"Do you have any plans to deal with your problems?"

"No. I can't think straight. I feel as if I am peering into a bottomless pit that's drawing me in, like it wants to consume me. Honestly, there's not a lot to live for."

"You can't continue to go on like this. Do you have any family?"

"No. We tried but it just didn't happen."

Sam had difficulty telling his story as tears kept welling in his eyes.

"I lost my wife from cancer two years ago. Now the disaster from the hurricane," he said.

He explained that he had a citrus plantation on 150 acres at Cranton on the Mississippi River about 60 miles north of New Orleans, and a big mortgage.

"My citrus trees and strawberry, blueberry and pecan crops are severely damaged as well as my house. I'm uninsured, and almost destitute."

Jack said he would like to see the property and the following weekend, when he at last had a couple of days off duty from the hospital, they drove in Sam's pick-up truck to Cranton.

Floods from the Mississippi and cyclonic winds had caused substantial damage to the citrus and other plantings. The house had been damaged by water intrusion through a missing section of the roof. Power was no longer connected but he had returned regularly to feed and milk a couple of dairy cattle in a paddock next to the house, and to feed the chooks that were now roaming through the house. There was a sad and eerie feeling about the scene and an odor of decay.

They walked to the packing and machinery sheds, which had sustained relatively minor damage, and then to the jetty on the river which had lost some of its flooring planks. Jack asked Sam what he thought the property was worth and how substantial his mortgage was.

His mind was racing, fired not only by a desire to help the down-caste man who stood next to him, who he felt genuinely sorry for. Here was also an interesting potential project that had suddenly arisen right in front of him.

When he arrived in New Orleans the thought of buying a property had not crossed his mind. His motivation to even consider purchasing the plantation was stimulated by multiple thoughts, including sympathy for Sam who he saw as a 'lost soul', as well as reflecting on the breakdown of his marriage. Although the situation with his broken marriage was not acrimonious, he was convinced that it was irretrievable.

In New Orleans there was also something of a 'lost soul' about Jack in his confused feelings and his uncertain view of a way ahead in life. He had experienced conflicting moods, doubts, and fears, as well as an urge sometimes to jump off into the 'unknown' – to start a new phase in his life.

Could this be the opportunity he had been looking for to lift his depressed feelings and rejuvenate himself? Some options might be opened-up. He felt he could potentially even create a break from his former life in New York and establish a new challenging, exciting, and refreshing way forward. He loved New York. He had never really lived anywhere else. His entire family and many of his friends lived there. Did that really matter if he was not happy? Maybe it was time for a change, far away from New York.

Somewhat impetuously, he made a generous offer to buy the property, to restore all the damage, including to Sam's house where he could continue to live, and to appoint him manager of the plantation.

'I will build a house on the property for myself, close to the river as a week-end getaway, and try living down south to see how life works out', he thought.

Sam was overcome with emotion by Jack's out-of-the-blue proposition and took some time to compose himself before they finally shook hands on the deal. On the drive back to New Orleans Jack asked what the plantation's name was. When he heard it did not have a name his quick response was: "Well, we will fix that right now, its name will be Gratton Grange."

CHAPTER 2

It was early evening as they drove from Cranton into the French Quarter. Sam asked Jack if he liked listening to live music.

"I learnt to play the piano while at med school in Washington DC. I'm a huge fan of jazz and blues music."

"Then let's go to Sirico's music venue on Bourbon Street for dinner, take in some of the best jazz in town, and listen to a brilliant songstress named Salina. I figure I can afford to go back there now."

"Done deal," replied Jack. "It can be a celebration of our new venture."

Over a dinner of oysters and a large bowl of local seafood Cajun style, washed down with a bottle of Napa Valley Pinot Grigio, they listened to *The Big Easy Band* five-piece jazz combo of drums, sax, clarinet, acoustic guitar and piano.

And then Salina appeared. She was a beautiful tall slim lightly-colored girl in her mid-twenties with a svelte figure clad in a long silver lame' dress – a picture of grace and elegance. Grabbing a mike, she launched straight into a powerful version of Louis Armstrong's *When The Saints Go Marching In* accompanied by singing and clapping from the enthusiastic audience.

This was followed by the classic *Summertime* in a complete change of mood and pace. The audience went silent as Salina moved in a slow sensuous glide, hips swaying, from one side of the stage to the other. Her voice had also changed, from a high-volume extrovert style to a wonderful soft, slightly husky, presentation.

Jack told Sam that during his piano lessons he learnt that the song was composed in 1934 by George Gershwin, with lyrics by DuBose Heyward, for the 1935 opera *Porgy and Bess*. He felt that its slow-moving style, containing elements of jazz and African American blues of the deep south, was perfect for a music venue in 'The Big Easy'.

Summertime, an' the livin' is easy
Fish are jumpin' an' the cotton is high.
Oh, yo' daddy's rich and yo' ma is good-lookin'
So hush little baby, don' you cry.

One of these mornin's you goin' to rise up singin'
Then you'll spread yo' wings an' you'll take to the sky.
But till that mornin', there's a nothin' can harm you
With Daddy an' Mammy standin' by.

During a break, Sam brought Salina across to their table where he introduced her to Jack and mentioned that he was a surgeon at the local hospital, a big fan of jazz and blues and an accomplished pianist. Soon after, he diplomatically excused himself to catch up with a friend at the bar.

Jack complimented Salina on her performance and how attractive she looked. He asked if she was born in New Orleans.

"I grew up in Montgomery, Alabama, and have only been in New Orleans for a couple of years. My mother Melissa was born in Paris of French Caucasian parents and met my father Raoul, who is an African American, when she visited New Orleans on a holiday. They own a small hardware and building supplies business in Montgomery and their products are in great demand for repair works following the hurricane."

Salina then said it was time to return to the stage and asked if he had a favorite song. He said he had several, but really loved *The Way You Look Tonight* which he had once heard Billy Holiday sing on tape. Salina smiled, took his hand and said: "Come and accompany me on the piano."

He felt embarrassed but went with her to meet the resident pianist who was quite happy to extend his break and listen to Jack play.

Salina lent on the side of the baby grand as Jack tickled the ivories and then, looking straight at him, she began to sing. Slowly she moved around and put a hand on his shoulder and then up onto his neck as she whispered: "Sing with me." The audience was silent as the duet proceeded and then burst into loud applause as he concluded with a dramatic pounding of the piano keys.

A couple of days later, Jack and Sam visited an attorney to arrange for registration of the name 'Gratton Grange', transfer of the property to Jack, and payout of Sam's mortgage to the bank. Jack then arranged for repairs to the house where Sam would be able to live rent-free and be paid a regular salary as manager of the plantation. His long-time field hand Joey would be retained plus a couple of other employees to assist in the general operation of the property. Work also commenced immediately to repair the damaged irrigation system and prune damaged citrus trees. Replacement plantings of citrus trees and of various other crops would also be undertaken as many rows had been swept away by flood waters.

Salina and Jack saw a lot of each other as the weeks flew by. Their relationship had quickly become close and their feelings quite intense. Sirico's was really buzzing again as tourists gradually returned to the French Quarter and Jack would visit there for dinner about once a week. On Salina's nights off they would have dinner at either his apartment or hers, and with her guidance he became something of an expert in Cajun-style cooking. One day they hired a power boat and travelled up the Mississippi to the Gratton Grange jetty for a picnic and to catch up with Sam, inspect restoration works, and have coffee at his restored house that he had moved back into.

While Jack discussed the direction for general management of the property with Sam, Salina went for a stroll amongst the citrus plantings. After walking along a row of lemon trees, she sat for a while in the shade of one and looked back at Sam's house.

After arriving in New Orleans from Montgomery and starting work at Sirico's, she had got to know Sam quite well with his friendly banter and sense of humor. Before the hurricane, he had told her a lot about his plantation, but she had never been there before. Then out of nowhere on that memorable night, he had introduced her to Jack who he had only recently met himself. Now, in the distance she could see them sitting in deep discussion on the verandah of Sam's house that Jack now owned.

How quickly the priorities in one's life could change she thought, feeling a sudden excitement as well as a little concern. Jack had become an important part of her life and, if she was honest with herself, she had already fallen in love with him.

Her thoughts drifted to what the future might hold if her relationship with Jack continued to develop. She wondered how compatible and well-matched they really were, and the extent to which lust might contribute to their attraction to each other. Salina saw him as a kind, thoughtful and trustworthy person. But while she appreciated his character and admired his intellect, she sometimes felt a sense of comparative inadequacy. Could a relationship between a mixed-race jazz singer and a sophisticated surgeon from New York really work out over the longer term?

As she gathered some lemons and walked back to the house, Salina decided to relax and go with the flow – 'what will be will be', she thought.

CHAPTER 3

In his quieter, pensive moments, Jack thought about the extent to which his life had changed. He had not only fallen in love with a local woman, but also with a revitalized New Orleans. Roots had been established in the area by purchasing a property – it was his new home.

Although he had some initial questions about how well Sam would adjust to no longer owning the plantation and becoming an employee, any concerns soon disappeared. Sam was proving to be capable, enthusiastic, and obviously grateful for what he called his 'second chance in life'. A virtual free reign was provided to him in managing the day-to-day operations and Jack ensured that he was involved in any major decision-making about future initiatives.

Returning to New York for a few days over Christmas and New Year to see his son Marcus, Jack also talked to Laura about a future education pathway for the boy. He also advised her of his desire to commence divorce proceedings.

He took Marcus ice skating in Central Park. They fed the squirrels and then walked to the Plaza Hotel for lunch where Charles the concierge extended a warm welcome and arranged for lemonade and pizza. Over lunch Jack talked to Marcus about how school was going and his relationship with Laura and her partner.

Marcus said he wanted to come live with Jack but was told that could happen later, that he must work hard at school for good grades and be a helpful son to his mother who loved him.

While in New York he settled the transfer of his interest in a medical clinic to his business partner Bryan Westerway, leased out his apartment on Long Island, and caught up with his parents Gordon and Maryanne.

Gordon was a retired director of a major stockbroking firm on Wall Street and proud of his son's achievements in the medical field. The Lansell's lived near Jack's apartment on Long Island in a large home with a swimming pool and tennis court. The property was ideal for entertaining. It was also close to Gordon's golf club and Maryanne's art classes.

His parents had anticipated his decision to settle permanently down south. He had kept them informed about the strong relationship that had developed with Salina. They were very keen to meet her and pleased that he was happy.

Jack's Porsche 911 sports, that he had purchased the previous Christmas as a present to himself, had been garaged at his apartment while he was in New Orleans. It was time to trade it on a new top-of-the-range Chevrolet SUV which would be more useful in operating the plantation.

The next day he began the long drive back to New Orleans in the SUV via Washington DC where he would catch up with his former lecturer in surgery at the George Washington University, Professor Harvey Janson. It was a cool but sunny day with a cloudless sky and while he missed the superb handling and acceleration of the Porsche, the Chevy provided plenty of power, space and comfort as he sped south on the New Jersey Turnpike and swung through Baltimore to Washington. Harvey was delighted to see him. They talked over lunch about the difficulties of rebuilding after the devastation in New Orleans and the challenges for Jack in juggling his work as a surgeon, in difficult conditions, and rejuvenating a damaged citrus plantation. Then it was on to New Orleans via overnight stays in Roanoke in Virginia and Birmingham in Alabama.

Soon after returning he briefed a local heritage architect to draw up plans for an impressive two-story plantation-style manor house. It would have five bedrooms, three bathrooms, wide verandah's upstairs and downstairs, fireplaces, a large sitting room with an adjoining dining room, a library and cellar, a spacious modern kitchen, and a wide grand staircase rising from the entrance hall.

There was a strategy evolving in his mind and it was becoming a driving force, which he was only just starting to recognize and submit to. Excited, he went back to work at the hospital but on arrival was quickly brought back to earth. Tom told him that he needed to immediately scrub-down to operate on a worker who had fallen several feet from an apartment balcony he was repairing, suffering multiple injuries.

Restoration works at Gratton Grange were now well advanced. The mature citrus trees that had been extensively pruned were looking refreshed and healthy, and the new berry and vegetable plantings were doing well. Crop growth was helped by the highly fertile alluvial soils of the flood plains along the Mississippi River. Sam had hired an engineer to inspect damage to the levees where Gratton Grange fronted the river and work had been undertaken to strengthen them.

Construction of the manor house was also moving along nicely with building materials regularly arriving both by road and river barge. The house had advanced to lock-up stage.

Jack's divorce from Laura was now finalized and whilst it was a strange feeling to suddenly realize that an important but difficult part of his life had drawn to a close, there was also eager anticipation about what the future might hold. The correctness of his decision to purchase Gratton Grange was reinforced as his relationship with Salina gathered strength and intensity.

CHAPTER 4

One Sunday during another picnic on the jetty, Jack and Salina watched the traffic on the river - some in a hurry and others just drifting along. She was looking to one side as a paddle steamer passed by on its way towards Baton Rouge with a big crowd on board. Jazz music floated across the water. Jack found himself staring at her profile and thinking how lucky he was to have such a wonderful woman in his life. He could not believe how much his own situation had changed over the last couple of years. It felt like he was living in a dream, that he hoped would never end.

At that moment he put his hand on her shoulder, turned her toward him, and asked her to marry him.

There was a silence that seemed to go on for a long time before she asked: "Are you sure?"

"I have never been more-sure of anything in my life. Will you marry me?"

"I feel somehow like we are meant to be together. You are a very caring and intelligent man, as well as strong and principled. I would love to be your wife."

He helped her up as the paddle steamer passed from view, hugged and kissed her. Then they just stared at each other, speechless.

They walked to Sam's house. He was the first to know, sat them down, produced a bottle of French Champagne and poured three glasses. "To the future mister and missus Lansell. What a great day," he said.

The next weekend they drove over 300 miles from New Orleans to Montgomery in Alabama to meet her parents Raoul and Melissa, and her brother Michael who worked in the family business. After lunch Jack took Raoul aside, told him that he loved his daughter, and asked his approval to marry her.

Raoul did not seem surprised. Over the last few months Salina had provided him and Melissa with a lot of information about the blossoming relationship. He had a good idea what was coming and did not hesitate to ensure Jack that he would be warmly welcomed into their family. They stayed the night and on Sunday set off early for the trip back to Gratton Grange.

Jack rang his parents to tell them the happy news and arranged for a local jeweler to design a solitaire diamond ring set on a plain gold band. He presented the ring to Salina at her apartment before they went to Sirico's, on her night off, for dinner with Tom and his wife Leanne. The appearance of Salina wearing the ring caused quite a stir with much clapping and congratulations. It was not long before a photographer and journalist arrived to prepare a story for the following day's edition of the New Orleans Gazette.

In the middle of Summer, they were married on board the Mississippi Princess paddle steamer by the captain. The entire boat had been hired for the event where some 200 guests were entertained including Salina's family from Montgomery and some of the family's closest friends, Salina's original singing and dance teacher from Montgomery, Jack's parents Gordon and Maryanne, his son Marcus, and his former clinic partner in New York, Bryan Westerway and his wife Jacinta. The manager of Sirico's was there, as well as Salina's friend Jessica who shared her apartment in New Orleans, Tom and Leanne and several staff from the hospital, Harvey Janson and his wife Patrice together with some of Jack's other friends from his university days in Washington.

The paddle steamer was decked out with balloons and streamers and music was provided by *The Big Easy Band*. Salina looked beautiful in a long white lace gown with a headpiece of white jasmine flowers and an alluring veil. The captain called the guests together and gave a brief introduction to the wedding ceremony about the joining together of two well-known local people who were obviously very much in love. Tom was best man and Sam was groomsman, while Jessica and Salina's sister Leah, who lived in Miami and worked as a tour guide, were bridesmaids. The bride was given away by her father who was a striking figure in a dinner suit as he walked his daughter down the short break that had formed through the crowd on the lower deck of the paddle steamer.

After Jack and Salina were proclaimed husband and wife a big cheer went up and copious quantities of French Champagne began to flow. Guests made their way to huge buffets of food prepared by Sirico's kitchen staff. The band played a variety of modern and trad jazz and at last Salina was persuaded to sing *What a Wonderful World* to much clapping and cheering. Late afternoon they docked at the Gratton Grange jetty where the happy couple stepped off to the accompaniment of congratulations, kisses and some tears from Salina's mother. Joey collected the couple in the plantation's motorized golf buggy and drove them to the manor house where they would stay overnight before leaving for a honeymoon in Paris. The Mississippi Princess turned and headed back to New Orleans with guest celebrations in full swing.

By this stage Jack was feeling the effects of a long and exciting day. He lay on the floor of the main living room and closed his eyes. Soon after he was startled by the hem of a white lace wedding dress brushing across his face. Looking up, there she was, standing over him as his eyes moved up those long legs to a white garter belt and the tops of her stockings where a small red rose was tucked, just below white silk camisole knickers.

He felt like he was in a dream or perhaps a Hollywood film but managed to say: "Oh, you are magnificent and that is the most beautiful flower that I have ever seen."

To which she replied: "Isn't it true that its often not what's on top that counts, so much as what's underneath?"

Trembling with excitement, he gasped: "Stop teasing and come to me Mrs. Lansell."

CHAPTER 5

They flew to New York and then on to Paris for two weeks where they stayed at an apartment on the Champs Elysée. Over breakfast they began to plan some activities but had a minor disagreement about Jack's suggestion to book a tour of Napoleon's luxurious residence Malmaison.

Jack was fascinated by the former emperor's exploits and what drove him. Salina said she believed he was nothing more than a dictator and warmonger whose armies had killed many people. Jack agreed that he had some significant faults but that in many ways he was a visionary conqueror who dismantled the feudal world of the Holy Roman Empire, abolished the Spanish Inquisition, and lifted many peasants from poverty. Also, he had encouraged capitalism to emerge as the guilds disappeared, and the Napoleonic Code was introduced to reform civil law.

Salina then suggested: "Why don't we do a deal – I will go with you to Malmaison if you will go with me to the Manet exhibition at the Grand Palais."

This was quickly agreed. Salina also mentioned that her aunt Claudette, who was her mother's sister and owned a café and music venue on the Left Bank, had suggested that they should visit the Folies Bergère before they departed Paris.

"Why don't I make a call and see if we can reserve a table for tonight," said Jack.

"Yes, that would be nice."

Jack picked up the phone and somehow managed to make a table reservation, despite the late notice, to see the Folies in the 9th Arrondissement.

Salina wanted to have her hair done so Jack arranged to visit the Notre Dame Hospital and checkout the latest developments in reconstructive surgery. After leaving the hairdresser's she wandered into a boutique near their apartment and bought two designer dresses - a smart black cocktail dress with a low scoop neckline, and a pretty ruby-red with a cut-on-the-cross skirt. Coming out of the boutique she noticed a young boy of about 12 years-of-age who smiled, walked up to her and said: "You look very lovely mademoiselle with your nice dress and seamed stockings, may I ask, are you wearing a garter belt?"

"Well young man," she responded in French, "That is for me to know and you to guess."

"I guess Yes."

He smiled again and walked away.

As she watched him disappear into the crowd Salina was amazed at the cheeky confidence of one so young. It was obvious that he was growing up very quickly. He certainly seemed to like ladies and appreciated feminine fashions. Maybe one day he might even become a fashion designer. 'Good luck to him', she thought.

Around 5.00 PM Jack returned to the apartment and realized that he had forgotten his key, so knocked gently on the door. There was no answer, so he knocked again. Slowly the door opened and there she was, stark naked except for red lipstick, a red necklace, red nails and red high heels.

She smiled meekly and said: "Hello, did you have a nice afternoon?"

"It was OK." he stuttered. "My lady in red, you are so beautiful."

He walked through the door and took her on the carpeted floor of the hallway as she whispered: "Don't mess-up my hair." An hour later they hurriedly dressed; he in a smart dark-grey business suit and silk tie, and she in the red dress that she had bought that afternoon.

Claudette had told her that the Folies Bergère cabaret music hall opened in 1872 and the revues featured extravagant costumes and sets with much near nudity of the performers. Josephine Baker, an expatriate African American singer and dancer caused a sensation when she appeared in just a skirt made of a string of artificial bananas. In 1882, Edouard Manet painted his classic *A Bar at the Folies Bergère* that featured a bar girl in front of a large mirror.

At a table close to the stage, Jack and Salina, sharing a large lobster salad and a bottle of Champagne, could not take their eyes off the continuing parade of exotic performances and dazzling sets.

Arriving back at their apartment after midnight they sat in the lounge and Jack poured them a gin and tonic nightcap before suggesting it might be time to get some sleep. Salina stood up, and let her red dress fall to the floor revealing a red garter belt, skimpy G-string and bra.

Then, with an impish look on her face, she turned to Jack and asked: "You like?"

"Oh yes, but where is the red rose?"

"It's in a little vase back at Gratton Grange, but I have a lovely pink frangipani for you."

She turned, bent over, slowly picked up her dress from the floor, and led him to the bedroom.

The next morning Jack stepped out of the shower, dried himself off, and came up behind her as she applied makeup in front of the mirror. He placed a hand on the curve of her bottom through the white satin dressing gown and asked: "How is the frangipani this morning?"

"Tingling." she said, suggesting he should stop, or they would miss the tour of Malmaison.

Touring through the stately building and grounds of the Chateau de Malmaison, Salina became impressed by the history of the property and the achievements of Josephine that the guide was explaining.

Josephine de Beauharnais had bought the manor house in 1799 for herself and her husband, General Napoleon Bonaparte, the future emperor of France. At the time it was a run-down estate of around 150 acres of woods and meadows which Josephine proceeded to transform into magnificent gardens featuring many rare and exotic plants and animals collected from around the world. A huge greenhouse was constructed and heated by coal-burning stoves, and animals that roamed around the grounds included kangaroos, emus, zebras, sheep, gazelles, ostriches, chamois, antelopes and llamas. Josephine died in 1814 and the Chateau became Napoleon's last residence in France after his defeat at the Battle of Waterloo in 1815 and his exile to the island of Saint Helena.

Following years of neglect, and destruction of most of the gardens during a battle in 1870, the Chateau was restored and was now well-maintained.

As they departed, Salina thanked Jack and told him she was pleased that he had encouraged her to go on the tour, although she was still not convinced that Napoleon was an honorable man.

Around midday they visited Salina's aunt Claudette for lunch at her café in the Latin Quarter on the Left Bank - the heart of Paris's bohemian culture with its vibrant café, art and music scene. A crowd had already gathered for lunch; indoors as well as alfresco on the sidewalk over-looking the Seine.

Claudette was delighted to see them, and especially pleased to meet Jack who she had heard so much about from her sister, Salina's mother in Montgomery. She introduced them to many of her customers, some of whom had become her close friends, and to the resident classical guitarist, Jerome, who was seated at a microphone in a corner of the spacious front room of the café. After a lunch of lightly pan-fried salmon in olive oil and a side salad, together with a fine bottle of Chablis from the cool climate Burgundy region, Salina was surprised to hear Jerome announce in a loud voice that a renowned jazz singer from New Orleans was present in the room. He invited her to join him at the microphone and with the enthusiastic encouragement of those around, Salina took a seat on a stool next to him.

She proceeded to sing Irving Berlin's *Blue Skies* in French, during which many people came in from the tables outside to listen to the performance. Many others who had been strolling by had gathered around the front of the cafe. She then did a joint rendition of *Let the Good Times Roll* with Jerome which brought the house down. She told the audience that the song was written in 1946 by Sam Theard, a New Orleans blues singer and song writer, in collaboration with Louis Jordan. She added that the song continued to be popular in New Orleans, and a common everyday saying.

Salina went back to a beaming Jack at their table and, as they ordered a couple of coffees, a line of people formed for her autograph. She also took several photos during the afternoon to send to her family and Jack's, as well as to Sam at Gratton Grange.

Later in the afternoon, as they walked to St-Germain, Jack said how proud he was of her.

"You are a woman of immense talent with an inner beauty and warmth that freely radiates to all those around you."

Tightening her grip on his hand, she turned towards him and quietly said: "I am so happy. I guess it shows, Dr Lansell. Coming from such different backgrounds we are so lucky that, with Sam's help, we found each other."

In St-Germain they wandered around the area's mixture of bohemian cafés and stylish shops where she bought a couple of nice tops, a light knit and a long silk wrap.

CHAPTER 6

Next day it was time to fulfill the other half of their agreement. They set off to see the Edouard Manet exhibition at the Grand Palais on the Champs Elysée.

It was an overcast day with light drizzle. They bought an umbrella from a vendor amongst the magnificent flower stalls that lined the boulevard and contributed some cash along the way to the numerous buskers. The whole scene, with the stylish fashions of the people and their multi-colored umbrella's, created a magical atmosphere in the 'city of light'.

Salina loved the impressionist masters. She explained to Jack that Manet was a modernist painter born in 1832 who died in 1883 and that his style of painting made a significant contribution in the movement from realism to impressionism.

"Jack, many of his paintings are of café scenes that reflect the social life of Paris in the 19th century. They especially capture the mood of Parisian nightlife. There is a mixture of bohemianism, urban working people and bourgeoisie in the scenes that he painted."

"I am looking forward Salina to viewing the exhibition. Also, as well as your knowledge of art, I am certainly impressed by this Grand Palais exhibition hall complex, with its large stone colonnades and enormous conservatory-style roof."

As they wandered through the exhibition, she suddenly grabbed his arm and whispered: "Jack, look, there is Manet's painting *A Bar at The Folies Bergère*. It is so beautiful. I can't believe that we are standing in front of it."

They then moved on to Manet's *Music in The Tuileries Gardens*. She stood and studied the painting for a long time, fascinated by the large leisurely crowd on the lawns and the fashions of the day. She could even imagine herself in that crowd, in a beautiful long dress, holding a parasol, and listening to the music.

She turned to Jack and said: "Maybe we should visit the Tuileries for a picnic tomorrow, what do you think?"

"Why not, tomorrow is expected to be a nice sunny day. We could obtain a basket of provisions at a market along the way."

As they left the exhibition, she noticed that full-size special edition numbered prints of some of Manet's paintings were for sale.

"I am going to buy one of that Folies Bergère painting, get it framed, and hang it at Gratton Grange as a memento of our honeymoon," she announced, scampering excitedly across to the sales desk in the foyer.

The next day was indeed sunny with a clear blue sky; like Salina had sung about in Claudette's café. Dressed in trim, slightly worn blue jeans that she had brought from home, white sneakers, a smokey-pink shirt she had bought in St-Germain, and a wide brimmed straw hat, she was in a joyous mood. Swinging her basket and almost skipping along. There was a young girlishness about her that he had not seen before, and it captivated him.

They walked down the Champs Elysée until they came to a small market stall where they bought some baguettes, cheeses, a chicken liver pate, a couple of apples, and two bottles of spring water which they placed in Salina's basket. Then they went on until reaching the Place de la Concorde in the 1st Arrondissement and entered the Tuileries Gardens.

The gardens, with colorful flower beds and many different types of trees, as well as fountains, sculptures and statues, stretched from the Place de la Concorde to the Louvre. It was a special place for people to stroll, meet, socialize and picnic. Manet's painting depicted a large group at a concert in the gardens near the Louvre.

Jack and Salina settled in the shade of a large tree on the lawn near a pond. Ducks cruised by and various other birdlife frolicked amongst the water lilies. Spreading a small tablecloth and setting out the food, they found that the walk, fresh air, and sunny day had stimulated their appetites.

After a while, when most of the food had been eagerly devoured, they relaxed and watched the passing parade of people along the nearby gravel pathway. There were all types of people. One might say an almost complete cross-section of society. Families with noisy but happy kids wandered by, as well as posers, singles, couples holding hands, couples not holding hands, together with the nicely dressed, overdressed, and the underdressed.

In her mind Salina had managed to reconstruct what the scene in Manet's painting might have been like all those years ago in the same gardens. She could almost hear the music, the chatter and the laughter of those people so long ago.

Jack observed her far-away look, put his arm around her and asked: "What are you thinking?"

"I believe those people in Manet's painting would have had a wonderful time here in these beautiful gardens, and so are we in our own way so many years later."

On the day before they left Paris, Jack told Salina he had made a booking at the Ritz Hotel for dinner the following night.

"Is that a good idea? I have heard it is quite expensive."

"I think we should do something special on our last night in this beautiful city. The Ritz is an institution in Paris with its reputation as a symbol of high society, luxury, service and fine dining. It is regarded as one of the leading hotels in the world. Over the years its clientele has included royalty, politicians, writers, film stars, and singers. The hotel has featured in several films, and in novels such as F Scott Fitzgerald's *Tender Is the Night* and Earnest Hemingway's *The Sun Also Rises*. Both writers often stayed at The Ritz and Hemingway's favorite bar is named after him. Also, the Duke and Duchess of Windsor stayed there after the royal abdication."

"I am convinced. It sounds like not only a great fine dining experience but also a step back into an important part of Parisian history."

Just after 7.00 PM Jack and Salina took a taxi to The Ritz where they were directed to the Hemingway Bar, with its rich wood paneling and leather upholstery, for a pre-dinner drink. Salina looked her usual elegant self in the black cocktail dress she had selected several days before at the boutique on the Champs Elysees.

Around the walls of the bar were numerous pictures, many taken by the novelist on his travels around the world, of people and places that attracted his attention and influenced his writing. Also on display was information about

Hemingway and his life. Salina, looking around the room, suddenly said to Jack:

"Come and read this. That Hemingway was a bit of a reckless fellow."

The piece that she was looking at told a story about how the famous novelist had stayed at the hotel many times after World War II. It was there that he learned his wife wanted a divorce. He reacted to the news by throwing her photo into a Ritz toilet and then shooting the photo and the toilet with his pistol.

Jack looked at her and said: "I am an admirer of Hemingway's writing but also know that he, like a lot of talented literary people, including F Scott Fitzgerald who was his sometime friend and drank with him in this very bar, had personality flaws. We should finish our drinks darling and move into dinner."

They walked down the long corridor of mirrors, old masters, and antique furniture to the L'Espadon restaurant. The maître 'd showed them to a table for two in a corner of the room. Every table was occupied and there was the muted sound of soft chatter and classical dinner music. The décor was opulent with high decorative ceilings, heavy plush drapes, flowers on every table and in large vases on pedestals around the room. There was a pleasant view through the large landscape windows to the floodlit gardens where a fountain gently flowed.

They were quickly attended to by a very polite waiter in an immaculately pressed black and white uniform. Both ordered oysters presented au la natural for entre while Salina ordered a coq au vin and Jack a medium rare fillet mignon for mains. A bottle of Merlot from the Bordeaux region was also selected. They finished with a shared plate of cheese, warmed olives, biscuits, and coffee. Salina took his hand across the table and thanked him for arranging a wonderful last night in Paris. It had given them a chance to relax, relive their experiences on the trip, and talk about some plans for the development of Gratton Grange when they returned.

CHAPTER 7

Arriving back in New York they arranged to stay for a couple of days with Jack's parents and catch up with his ex-business partner Bryan Westerway and his wife Jacinta. They took a cab to Long Island where they received a warm welcome from Gordon and Maryanne and were delighted to learn that Marcus was also staying there with his grandparents. When Jack introduced him to Salina the young boy took her extended hand and shyly said: "I am very pleased to meet you," before they all moved inside so that the travelers could shower and change clothes.

Over a light lunch under a large umbrella beside the pool they talked about the wonderful time the newly-weds had in Paris, including the visit to Claudette at her café. Jack also outlined some of the plans they had for Gratton Grange. Gordon announced that he had made a reservation for lunch the following day at the Long Island Country Club where he had been a member for many years.

As the conversation swung to the current shows on Broadway and the latest women's fashions in New York, Gordon took an increasing interest in the vibrant personality that Salina projected. The only time he had met her previously was briefly during the wedding celebrations on the Mississippi paddle steamer.

She was certainly very physically attractive, but he also saw an intellectual sharpness on display that he was not expecting. One minute she was listening intently to Maryanne, then offering considered responses, before suddenly reacting with a burst of laughter at a comment made by Maryanne about the lack of any fashions on the models at her life-sketching art classes.

'This is a woman with a multi-faceted personally – it is impossible to not like her, she seems to virtually pick people up and carry them along with her,' he thought. He observed the way she looked at people with a warm intensity, indicating an obvious interest in what they are saying and encouraging them to continue.

Gordon also noted the happy and relaxed relationship between Salina and Jack, although their personalities were quite different. Salina was effervescent and demonstrative while Jack tended to be reserved and thoughtful - more like his father. He felt it was an excellent combination.

Previously, returning home after the wedding down south, Gordon had asked Maryanne whether she thought the marriage of a white man with a mixed-race woman could be an issue for some people.

"That has not even crossed my mind, and it certainly is not an issue for us. They are obviously happy and very much in love – that should be enough to put any doubter's minds at rest," Maryanne had said, quickly changing the conversation.

Now, sitting opposite from Salina beside the pool, Gordon suddenly realized that he was staring at her and adjusted his gaze to the side, looking out over the garden. Music could be heard floating through the open doors from the sitting room behind them.

Salina had been conscious that Gordon had been quietly checking her out. Now she decided to draw him out for a better understanding of his personality.

"Gordon, you have good taste in music. That is Sarah Vaughn with her hit song, *Misty*. She is one of the greatest jazz singers of all-time with a voice that projects and flows easily, with enormous vitality, and a richness of genuine emotion. I think at times her voice sounds like a musical instrument, especially the violin."

Salina immediately went up several more levels in Gordon's estimation. He was not only impressed with her knowledge of music, but also flattered by her compliment to him.

"You are right Salina. Sarah is one of my favorite jazz performers, as well as yourself of course. I have not forgotten your moving rendition of *What a Wonderful World* on board the Mississippi Princess."

"Thank you, Gordon. Tell me, now that you are retired as a stockbroker, do you still dabble in shares? I know very little about the stock market, but a customer at Sirico's once told me that he had made a lot of money by investing in shares."

"I still hold a substantial portfolio that I spend some time most days managing. One can certainly make a good profit, but it's also possible to experience a significant loss. I stay away from speculative stocks and focus on blue chip companies within a broad spread of industries. Earlier, I looked for higher growth in my investments, but today my portfolio is diversified across medium growth stocks with lower risk. If some time you wish to consider investment in the stock market, I will be pleased to give you some advice on how to go about it and provide suggestions about what stocks to invest in."

"I would like to talk to you one day about that. Jack, we have never discussed investing in shares. Do you own any?"

"Just a small portfolio that my father helped me establish some years ago, and which continues to grow quite nicely. My main interest now is in property and especially the future development of Gratton Grange, but there is no reason why you could not also start a portfolio of your own. We can talk about that."

"Every day my view of the world seems to get broader and more exciting. I had never even thought about being an investor in shares."

Gordon smiled and glanced across at Jack with a look of encouragement. He was pleased by Salina's interest in his former career and the opportunity to provide some advice about the stock market.

Maryanne asked Salina if she would like to see some of her sketches and paintings. She took her hand as they walked inside.

Almost effortlessly it seemed, Salina had won the hearts of Jack's parents with her bubbly outgoing personality, her sincerity, and her enquiring mind.

Next day on the way to the Country Club in Gordon's Mercedes, which Maryanne claimed he always drove too fast, Salina commented on the great number of beautiful homes on Long Island and the generally peaceful and healthy atmosphere of the whole area. Gordon had arranged for a window table in the clubhouse overlooking the first tee and the wide fairway lined on each side with a variety of attractive trees and bushes. They could receive table service or opt to cook their own steaks on the outside barbeque and select from the extensive salad bar. Salina said she would like to cook a steak and a sausage on the barbeque which Marcus thought was a terrific idea. The others ordered from menus that a waiter provided.

Having selected a couple of prime scotch fillet steaks, Salina and Marcus went out to a barbeque where she asked him how he liked his steak done.

"Not too raw," he said.

"How does medium rare sound?"

"That sounds alright."

"OK, two medium rare steaks coming up."

They let the steaks sizzle for a while, turning them once, before Salina lightly sliced into one and asked: "How about that?"

"Perfect," he said, and they did high fives.

After lunch Gordon suggested they wander outside to one of the practice greens and check out their putting skills. With some putters and balls that Gordon had obtained from his locker in the clubhouse they took turns sinking puts from various areas of the green. This quickly developed into a keen competition, but with lots of ribbing and laughter.

Arriving back at the home of her new in-laws, Salina commented on the lovely garden that Maryanne and Gordon had created, when Marcus interrupted.

"I have a garden here too."

To which Salina responded: "Why don't you show me".

He took her by the hand as they walked around the swimming pool and through a gate in a hedge to a hidden garden area. He explained that the section on the right was Maryanne's herb garden and on the left was his vegetable plot that included a small bed of petunias and azaleas in flower.

"Do you also have a garden at home," she asked.

"No, because we live in an apartment. We do have some pot-plants on our balcony, but nothing like this. That is why I really like coming here and looking after my garden. Do you have a garden at home?"

She told him about the garden she planned at Gratton Grange and asked him what he wanted to do when he grew up.

"I want to be a farmer," he said emphatically without hesitation.

"Well, keep working hard at school and that could happen."

Early the next day Gordon drove Jack and Salina to the airport for the flight back to New Orleans. On the way they dropped Marcus off to his mother at their apartment in Brooklyn where Marcus said goodbye to his father and received a kiss on the cheek from his new friend Salina. Laura came out with a smile to say hello to Jack and to meet Salina for the first time.

CHAPTER 8

A rriving at their new home at Gratton Grange they met with Sam. Salina presented him with a large beautifully illustrated book on the history of the Folies Bergère. She also showed him the Manet print she had bought in Paris and asked him if he could arrange for Joey, who was a competent artisan, to frame it.

They then discussed the future development and operation of Gratton Grange. Following the loss and damage of many citrus trees to the hurricane, and the much smaller harvest expected as the fruit ripened, Sam suggested that they focus just on supplying the main local areas including New Orleans and Baton Rouge, plus Cranton. Those markets were now starting to recover with the arrival of more tourists. New citrus plantings would not mature for some time, so they would rely on existing citrus and new plantings of vegetables and pecans to help replace lost income.

Jack agreed with the strategy but added that he wanted to upgrade the general presentation of Gratton Grange by initiatives such as improved access by road and river. New signage would be installed at the entrance from the main road as well as at the jetty on the river. The main driveway would be refurbished, together with the short branch driveway to the manor house that would culminate in a circular design that included a fountain surrounded by a rose garden. The existing access to the jetty would be widened to form an extension of the main driveway, with extensive landscaping down each side. Produce from the property could then be easily dispatched from both main exits – via road and the river.

Salina said she wanted to establish beautiful gardens and sweeping lawns at the front of the manor house overlooking the river. She also wanted to continue singing at Sirico's, but only on one night per week. Sam said he would arrange for a backhoe to prepare the ground for the gardens and lawns, plus obtain quotations for the works that Jack wanted.

Over the previous spring and summer Sam had fertilized the orange, lemon, mandarin, and grapefruit trees. Spraying had also been undertaken to control pests such as citrus leaf miner moths that lay eggs on the underside of new growth. Harvesting of the fruit, utilizing contract labor, commenced in late September and continued until January. New plantings of citrus varieties to replace those damaged by the hurricane, plus introduction of some new lemon and lime trial plantings, was planned for January and February.

That year, as in the past on the property, all citrus harvesting was done by hand. Jack thought that this was acceptable in view of the much smaller harvest. However, he planned to ask Sam to check out the cost and benefits of introducing mechanical harvesting for future crops.

Salina eagerly sought a variety of plants from local nurseries for her new gardens including colorful phlox, hibiscus, azaleas, magnolia, iris and, of course, a frangipani. She also obtained some blue wisterias with their attractive grape-like bunches of flowers. These would be trained up the pillars at the front of the house so that they could spread across the upstairs verandah and create a spectacular display. Some would also be planted to grow up the pergola that covered the deck at the back of the house. And she had begun attending a gardening class at the Louisiana Horticulture Institute in New Orleans.

One afternoon, clad in jeans, a denim shirt, boots, and gardening gloves, she was working in her new garden at the front of the house when Sam walked by and said he had finished reading the book that she gave him on the Folies Bergère.

"That black dancer and singer, Josephine Baker, sure was some girl. I will never eat another banana without thinking of her," he said.

"From all accounts, she was a great dancer and singer, and a hot lady. You are a funny man Sam. I must be sure to have a banana plant in my gardens."

They both laughed loudly, and Salina suddenly exclaimed: "Now look what you made me do. I've knocked over the liquid fertilizer container."

"Don't worry, everything will grow like crazy now."

"Sam, look at all the bees that the flowers are attracting. I have also noticed that they love the flowers on the citrus trees. Bees are important for cross pollinating crops and for our ecology generally, although not for citrus crops because those flowers have both male and female components, so they do their own pollinating."

"How do you know all that?"

"I read about it because I love bees and would like to be an apiarist. I could provide beehives to give them good homes and harvest their honey to sell."

"Well, why don't you do it? There is a Beekeepers Club in Cranton. I will introduce you to the president, Delice. You would learn a lot about setting up and operating an apiary from those people."

Sam was impressed. This was just another example of the growing interest that Salina was showing in what life could be like on a plantation and the opportunities that were there.

It was winter and southern Louisiana was getting quite cold at night. Sitting in the lounge in front of the fire, Jack quietly suggested to Salina, as she read a book on cultivating roses: "I think we should invite your folks over soon and show them what we are doing here with the development of Gratton Grange."

"Oh, that would be nice, Michael could look after their business for a few days while they are here. I will phone them now."

After an excited discussion with her mother, Salina told Jack that they would love to come the weekend after next.

When they arrived Salina proudly showed her mother around the developing gardens. She explained in French how she also planned to start an apiary. Jack took Raoul on a tour of the plantation. Approaching the boundary on the southern border of the property Jack pointed to the cotton crop of his neighbor, Cooper. When he commented on how he would like to purchase that property if the opportunity arose, he noticed a wistful smile cross Raoul's face.

"That would please Sam as he told me when I was talking to him this morning that he does not like Cooper, who believes that black people should not run a plantation."

To which Jack angrily responded: "Racists like Cooper are a disgrace and certainly should not be managing people."

Raoul then told Jack in an emotional voice about how his ancestors were shipped to America and sold at a slave market in Montgomery to the master of a large cotton plantation in Alabama.

He explained that cotton was the leading crop across most of the southern states during the first half of the 19th century and slaves became the most common form of labor.

"Invention of the cotton gin by Eli Whitney encouraged the growing of cotton, and the use of slaves. Today it is hard to imagine the terrible sub-human way in which they were often treated on the plantations. It involved horrendous abuse, cruelty and even lynching's. By around 1860 Alabama had more than 400,000 slaves and was a center for the slave trade due to easy access by railroads and the Alabama River."

Trying to comfort him, Jack put a hand on his shoulder.

"Thankfully, those terrible days are now long gone, although there is still significant room for improvement in the socio-economic situation of many black people in this country," he said.

CHAPTER 9

S oon after her parents returned to Montgomery, Sam took Salina to a late afternoon meeting of the Cranton Beekeepers Club at Delice's property just north of the city.

Meetings of the club, which had about 10 members, were bi-monthly and alternated around members properties. Discussions covered a wide range of topics such as effective and efficient operation of apiaries and market conditions for honey products. Salina was warmly welcomed as a potential new member and was fascinated by the various aspects of the industry that were discussed. She learnt that high quality honey is produced in Louisiana, but it soon became apparent that a significant investment was necessary upfront to start a small apiary. Profit should only be expected after the second or third year.

The meeting lasted nearly two hours after which Delice took Salina aside and offered to arrange for the supply of a few hives with queens and worker bees, associated equipment such as a smoker, together with protective clothing including a head-to-toe suit and gloves.

Arriving home at about 7.00 PM just in front of Jack, she told him about her visit to the beekeepers meeting and that she would like to start a small apiary at Gratton Grange. Her plan was that it would commence more as a hobby and gradually mature into a commercial operation over two to three years. She wanted to know what he thought of the idea and would he agree to providing funds for establishment.

"I am impressed with your budding entrepreneurial spirit, but not surprised - you are much more than just a beautiful woman. Certainly, you should proceed. The funds can come from our joint operating account."

She jumped up with a joyous squeal, threw her arms around him, and kissed him repeatedly. While dinner was cooking, she phoned Delice and told her to go ahead with arranging the necessary requirements for her new project.

Over dinner Jack spoke about the need to set up appropriate structural and financial arrangements to deal with the future development of Gratton Grange.

"I think that we will soon need to see our accountant about setting up Gratton Grange as a company. We don't want to be the biggest around here, but we need to be the most efficient and forward looking," he said.

The next day she drove in her new Honda SUV to the Louisiana Horticulture Centre to discuss suitable rose varieties to grow in the Cranton area. She was advised that blackspot and powdery mildew were challenges in growing roses in hot and humid conditions. It would be best to go for landscape shrub roses in her plantings. These varieties had low water and pruning requirements, and less insect susceptibility. On the way home she called into a specialist nursery and ordered two dozen shrub roses, with a range of colors, to be delivered.

The large three-level fountain that formed a central feature in the circular garden at the manor house had recently been installed and plumbing works completed. Salina could now proceed with planting the roses around the fountain together with lots of azaleas to provide a blaze of color. In garden beds that she created each side of the main entrance to the house, fronting the river, she planted a frangipani on one side and a magnolia on the other, and at each corner of the house, a banana plant.

Soon after, the requirements to establish the apiary arrived and then Delice visited to help Salina, together with Sam, select a suitable site for the new enterprise and set up the hives. Delice said she would also arrange for one of her field hands to instruct and work with Salina during the early stages of the project.

One night during dinner at Sirico's, just after Salina had finished singing a couple of songs, they noticed that the captain of the Mississippi Princess and his wife were also there. He came across and asked if she was interested in doing a one-off guest appearance during a Sunday afternoon cruise. She and Jack could board the steamer at the Gratton Grange jetty and be delivered back there on return from Baton Rouge.

"Oh, I would be delighted to do that. The Sunday after next?"

"Agreed," said Bernard. "We are once again experiencing heavy bookings for our cruises. There will be a four-piece band, and Jack might like to accompany you on the piano."

A couple of weeks later the Mississippi Princess slowed as it approached the Gratton Grange jetty where it briefly stopped, scattering some resident pelicans and other assorted bird life. Jack helped Salina aboard where they were welcomed by Bernard. They then had a light lunch with him before he introduced Salina, dressed casually in white slacks and a loose-fitting bright floral top, as the feature artist for the afternoon. He told the crowd of tourists on board from around the world that she was a regular performer at Sirico's in New Orleans and had also sung recently at a music venue in Paris.

After several songs, Jack joined her on the piano. They finished with Hoagy Carmichael and Ned Washington's *The Nearness of You*. It was an unforgettable performance with Salina standing close to Jack, looking into his eyes, and swaying slowly to the music.

Some couples who had been dancing on the small dancefloor stopped and just watched the sensual performance. One woman even shed a tear.

A lady in the audience whispered to her friend: "There is something going on between those two," to which her friend responded: "I heard they are married."

"Well, all I can say is that they must be very much in love to be able to perform together like that. It is beautiful to see."

The audience clapped and cheered for a long time as Salina and Jack held hands, bowered, and nodded in appreciation of the acclaim. As they stepped back onto the jetty at Gratton Grange, the passengers moved to that side to wave them goodbye, and as the paddle steamer moved out into the middle of the Mississippi to return to New Orleans, Bernard released a couple of blasts from the engine steam whistle.

Soon after, over dinner one night, Salina told Jack that she had been to see her doctor in New Orleans as she had been feeling a little unwell.

"So, what was his diagnosis?"

"He said I am pregnant."

"Gosh, what wonderful news."

"You are happy?"

"Darling, I could not be happier. We are going to be a family."

She raced to tell Sam and then phoned her parents in Montgomery who were ecstatic to hear that they would become grandparents. Jack's parents in New York were also over the moon at the anticipated arrival of another grandchild to join Marcus. Melissa and Maryanne both spoke to Salina with advice about dealing with the pregnancy and looking after the new arrival. The news spread quickly. Cards and emails rolled in, as well as lots of phone calls.

As the pregnancy progressed, Jack suggested that because their parents did not live near-by they should employ a live-in housekeeper-nanny to assist Salina. This could be an ongoing long-term arrangement which would also enable her to progressively return to looking after her garden and apiary. She agreed and was very appreciative of his thoughtfulness and understanding.

Jack was in the process of establishing his own consulting clinic in New Orleans that would specialize in reconstructive surgery. He planned to continue performing operations at the New Orleans Medical Centre, but also at other hospitals in the area. After renting premises in the Warehouse District on the edge of the French Quarter, he invited a young black surgeon to join the new clinic as a junior partner.

Dr Julian Canning had been recommended by Professor Harvey Jansen in Washington who advised that he had a good grasp of the latest developments in reconstructive surgery, including skin grafts following major burn injuries, and micro-surgery relating to nerve damage in severely damaged limbs. He said he was friendly, extremely competent, and would be a valuable partner in the new consulting business.

After an initial meeting, Jack took Julian around town and introduced him to key people in the various hospitals, including Tom Eustace at the New Orleans Medical Center and several general practitioners. On one day they travelled to hospitals in Baton Rouge and another in Cranton before dinner at Gratton Grange where Julian met Salina for the first time. She later told Jack that she liked the cut of his new partner, that they should work well together, and that the arrangement was important to provide cover for Jack when he took time off occasionally for a holiday.

Eloise Lansell arrived, with Jack present - a healthy 8lb baby on schedule in a natural birthing at the New Orleans Medical Centre. She looked like a little

Salina with her dark hair and light olive complexion. She had a voice, that Jack jokingly suggested to the midwife, could maybe develop into that of an opera singer one day.

Beth, a former nurse in her early sixties, had been appointed housekeeper at Gratton Grange and was now able to assist Salina with the needs of the new arrival. She was perfect for the role with her nursing background. An added benefit was that she was also a good cook. Private and spacious living quarters had been prepared for Beth in a downstairs corner of the house, and Jack had arranged for her to be paid a generous remuneration.

CHAPTER 10

C itrus harvesting had been successfully completed and the produce dispatched to supermarkets in New Orleans, Baton Rouge and Cranton. Some also went to a processor in Baton Rouge for fruit juice production. The eye-catching boxes carried the Gratton Grange trademark and logo. Additional plantings of orange, mandarin and grapefruit trees were now well advanced as well as the trial plantings of new lemon and lime varieties.

Then an event occurred that would have a major impact on the future direction of Gratton Grange. Cooper Bradley, who was in his early seventies, died suddenly of a heart attack. His wife had passed away eight years earlier, but he had an industrial chemist daughter who lived in Atlanta, and a son was an army officer based in Dallas. The Cranton Chronicle carried an article on Cooper's death and there was a notice in the classified section that a funeral would be held in New Orleans in four days.

Jack met with Sam to discuss the upcoming funeral, which he felt he should attend as a neighbor, but he understood when Sam said he did not wish to go. He told Sam he was interested in purchasing the property if it became available for sale, and that he would seek to discuss the matter with Cooper's son and daughter. An estimate of the value of Cooper's property was now needed urgently.

Early the following morning an estimate from a certified valuer in the Warehouse District of New Orleans was obtained by Jack before he arrived at the main hospital to perform a scheduled operation.

Around midday he left the hospital for two hours before he was due back for another operation. In his mind he was considering the best way to move forward with his interest in buying Cooper's property. He was keen not to be seen as a go-getter taking advantage in an unfortunate situation, so there was a need to make a reasonable offer, to show genuine consideration for the bereaved, and to ensure that Cooper's employees were properly looked after if he purchased the plantation.

He headed for a nearby café and took a seat at a small table, under a canvas awning near the front entrance, where he ordered a ham and salad wrap and a bottle of mineral water. The previous occupant of the table had left a copy of the New Orleans Gazette which he started flicking through. On page five he came across an article about Cooper Bradley's family history that included a photo of Cooper with his son and daughter. The café was already crowded with people having lunch. At a table nearby he overheard two ladies discussing Cooper.

"That guy Cooper, he was a strange one. You know, he used to come in here sometimes, but I never saw him smile, not once. Always grumpy and I believe he was a very tough boss to the men on his plantation up there near Cranton. He won't be a loss to the community."

"That's a bit harsh Glenis. He lost his wife just a few years ago and I understand his children have moved away and now live interstate. I have heard that some people regarded him as a bit of a racist, but you can't just go on gossip and believe everything you hear. I suspect he was probably a lonely old man when he died. I wonder what will happen to his property?"

Jack continued to read the article on Cooper. It was reported that his father was killed in the Second World War when Cooper was only six. His mother brought him up at the same time as she struggled to run the plantation with the help of hired labor. Then, a couple of years later, he contracted polio. Muscle weakness, caused by the disease, resulted in one leg being shorter than the other and requiring him to wear a leg brace and a special elevated boot for the rest of his life. Jack guessed this would account for the slight limp that he had noticed when he last saw Cooper.

The article also revealed that over several years Cooper had been a significant financial contributor to the operations of the Louisiana Agriculture Centre. In addition, it said he had gifted substantial funds to the main hospital where he had received ongoing medical attention relating to his affliction, including occasional bouts of severe depression. Jack looked intently at the photo in the paper. Both children were smiling broadly but Cooper looked quite serious, with an almost glum expression. 'He certainly does not look like a happy man', thought Jack. 'I should avoid forming a firm opinion about the character of someone I only met once or twice and hardly knew at all.'

He gazed out at the large walnut tree which formed a centerpiece for the café's outdoor area. It was covered in lush new growth after being battered by the hurricane. The tree had looked like a skeleton when he first started work at the hospital after arriving from New York. Now it had sprung back to life, much like he had after meeting Salina. Many birds were flying around chirping or resting on the branches, and two tiny sparrows picked at the leftover bits of his lunch, from the plate that he had pushed to the edge of his table for them.

Thinking about the conversation he had just overheard, Jack reflected on something that his mother had once said to him, in response to a question he had asked as a young boy as they walked down a street in Manhattan.

Passing a homeless man camped in a doorway with all his worldly belongings, Jack asked: "Mother, why is that smelly man with dirty clothes permitted to sit there like that in front of everyone passing by?"

"Jack, we do not know what difficulties that man may have faced in life that brought him to this awful situation. One should never judge a book by its cover."

As he got up to leave the cafe, Jack fought back an impulse to go over to the women and suggest that Cooper had apparently led a rather difficult life and they should not jump to conclusions about the type of person that he had been. However, not wanting to get involved in a conversation that he felt was really none of his business, and being due back at the hospital, he kept walking.

CHAPTER 11

S itting in the back row at the funeral parlor chapel, Jack watched as about sixty people filed in and took their seats. Cooper's children sat in the front row and as the organ music subsided his son Greg rose and went to the rostrum where he was joined by his sister Allison. She stood beside him as he began an emotional eulogy to his father. He told how his family were third-generation owners of the plantation. His father had been a strict disciplinarian as he and his sister grew up and went to school and college in New Orleans. Nevertheless, they loved him and appreciated that they were well provided for in a material way. Greg said that his father had encountered significant challenges in his life and never got over the death of their mother, which caused his mental and physical health to deteriorate over recent years.

After the service Jack sought out Greg and Allison and introduced himself. He offered his condolences, gave them his business card, and said that if there was any way that he could assist at that difficult time to not hesitate to contact him. A few days later Greg rang him and asked if they could meet for lunch at a café in the French Quarter.

Over lunch Greg explained that his father's property had been willed to himself and his sister. She had now left town to attend to her business in Atlanta. However, she had suggested that he talk to Jack about the possible sale of their fathers' plantation and give him first option. She also gave her brother authority to negotiate a sale and sign any related documents on her behalf. Greg added that he was aware that his father had not always been an easy person to relate to but that they would like to see the property pass to an owner who would look after it and run it effectively. Finishing his coffee, Jack said he was keen to extend the acreage at Gratton Grange to provide a more diversified and economically viable operation.

"How much would you and Allison want for the property?"

"We obtained a sworn valuation before Allison left yesterday which includes all buildings, machinery and equipment," Greg said, sliding a document across the table to Jack.

"That is slightly above what I had in mind, but I will accept your valuation and raise it by the cost of your reasonable legal expenses for the transaction."

They both smiled, shook hands, and ordered two glasses of Napa Valley Shiras to celebrate. Greg rang Allison to convey the news while Jack rang Salina.

Greg told Jack he had been granted four weeks leave from the army and planned to spend the time at his late father's property. Jack then phoned his lawyer to arrange a meeting for the following day, which would include a New Orleans lawyer formerly used by Cooper. He then went to a meeting with his bank manager, who said he was familiar with the current valuation of Cooper's property and assured him that finances would be in place to enable purchase.

The following afternoon Jack and Salina met with Greg and the lawyers together with a representative from the bank where the relevant documents were signed to arrange for transfer of the property from Coopers' estate to Jack and Salina. It was agreed that steps would be taken to fast-track probate and that settlement would be in sixty days. As they left the meeting, Greg said he would arrange for Cooper's personal effects to be removed, and he invited Jack and Salina to join him for a general inspection of the property. Jack thanked him and it was agreed that they would be accompanied by Sam.

During the tour of the property Sam said he understood that about 50 percent of the total 350 acres was under cotton, about 25 percent consisted of various vegetable and citrus plantings, and the remainder lay fallow. Firstly, they inspected the cotton crop which had been planted by Cooper. It would require fertilizing and irrigation, as well as weed and insect control prior to harvesting. Jack commented that resources would need to be immediately available to enable these requirements to be effectively undertaken. They needed to ensure that the existing field hands stayed on, and he would like Sam to talk to them the following day, which was agreed.

They then moved on to look at the vegetable crops and citrus trees which seemed to be progressing well, and then to inspect the machinery and buildings including Cooper's house. The colonial style single-story timber house had four-bedrooms and was about 30 years old. It appeared in reasonable condition but needed some refurbishing, as well as cleaning and painting. Salina was quick to note that the kitchen and bathroom could be updated and that the garden was overgrown and in need of attention.

Back at Gratton Grange, Sam questioned the future of cotton growing on Cooper's property. He said that cotton growing had been increasingly concentrated in the northeast of Louisiana and that other crops were preferred in the south.

"The cotton industry is faced with many significant challenges including strict environmental regulations which means that less-effective pesticides are now being used. There is also increased competition from overseas producers as well as from synthetics. I believe there is better revenue potential in other uses of the land, including extension of citrus and vegetable growing."

"As well as beekeeping," added Salina.

"And maybe that too," said Sam.

"I have been looking at the current situation in relation to cotton growing and the projected outlook, especially in this area of Louisiana, and I agree with you Sam," responded Jack.

So, the current cotton crop would be their last and they would commence planning the way ahead for an expanded, more diversified, and cost-effective Gratton Grange.

Prior to meeting with the field hands at Cooper's, Sam briefed Joey about the pending purchase of Cooper's property and that it would become part of the Gratton Grange operations. He also appointed him as the leading hand with authority to work across all operations and said he wanted him to also attend the meeting at Cooper's.

At a table in Cooper's house, with Cooper's son Greg seated beside him, Sam introduced himself as general manager at Gratton Grange, and Joey as the leading hand. He then addressed the four permanent field hands that had worked for Cooper and explained that, when the purchase of the property was finalized, they would be merged with the two currently employed at Gratton Grange to form a team of field hands led by Joey.

He then invited each man in turn to speak about their field experience, the type of work that each preferred, and whether they had any questions. They all seemed to be generally happy with the proposed new arrangements. But one asked if they would be able to offer suggestions occasionally if they saw opportunities to improve operations, as this had not been the case with Cooper. Sam was pleased with the question and said that new ideas would certainly be encouraged, openly discussed, and evaluated.

At the end of the meeting Sam thanked Greg for the opportunity to talk to the men. As Sam and Joey left, they overheard one of the field hands comment on what a change it would be to soon have a black man in charge at Cooper's property, and another black man as leading hand, instead of the rather terse style of Cooper.

Driving the short distance back to Gratton Grange, Sam remarked to Joey: "That went quite well. I think we can look forward to a friendly and productive relationship with those men."

"It's like a new exciting era is opening up before us, mostly due to the leadership and progressive attitudes of Jack and Salina. Thank you, Sam, for my promotion and the faith that you are showing in my ability, I will not let you down."

The transaction went smoothly to settle the sale of Cooper's property. As they shook hands Greg, in a rather dramatic moment, presented the keys to Cooper's former home to Jack and Salina and expressed his best wishes. On behalf of himself and Salina, Jack thanked him for such an easy hand-over and told him that he was always welcome to visit if ever he was in the area.

CHAPTER 12

Arriving home in the early evening, the proud owners of an expanded Gratton Grange opened a bottle of Verve Clique Champagne and invited Sam and Joey in to celebrate. Beth served a cheese and biscuits platter and then joined them at the table before going to bath Eloise and prepare her for bed.

Jack took the opportunity with Sam and Joey there to outline the plans that he and Salina had to incorporate Gratton Grange, and that he and Salina would be directors. He also invited Sam to become a director of the new company and, following his appointment to leading hand, offered Joey a profit-sharing arrangement as part of a new remuneration package. In addition, Jack said they planned to refurbish Cooper's former house and asked Sam if he would like to live there as it would be more central to the overall operations of Gratton Grange. He also indicated that if Sam would like to move, then his current house would be offered to Joey so that he would no longer need to travel from his rented apartment in Cranton.

Sam was quick to indicate his agreement to the proposal, and mentioned that his relationship with Belinda, who was an African American and worked in administration at Cranton Fruit Juice, was now quite close. She might join him in living at the refurbished house. The broad smile on Joey's face clearly showed how pleased he was to take up the offer that was made to him.

Following completion of the renovations, Sam and Belinda moved into Cooper's former house. A modern electronics-based office was set up where she would be able to assist him in bookkeeping and general administration relating to the expanded operations of Gratton Grange.

How ironic - the twists and turns of fate. The black man who had been told by Cooper that a black man should never manage a plantation was now managing Cooper's former plantation. Also, he would be living with his new black partner in Cooper's house.

Sam did not see this as some sort of vengeance, but rather a pathway to build on the opportunity given to him by Jack at their chance meeting after the devastation wrought by the hurricane. The depression and helplessness that he felt just prior to meeting Jack reminded him somewhat of the famous lines in Shakespeare's *Hamlet* that he had studied in English class at high school:

> *"To be or not to be, - that is the question:*
> *Whether 'tis nobler in the mind to suffer*
> *The slings and arrows of outrageous fortune*
> *Or to take arms against a sea of troubles,*
> *And by opposing end them?"*

Sam sometimes found it hard to believe how much his fortunes had changed and how much happier he was now. His confidence was restored in his abilities, and he could clearly see a more prosperous road ahead.

He had learnt that tomorrow is another new day. The sun will again come up and shine a clearer and more encouraging light on the way forward, much as it did for Raoul's forebear's when they were freed from slavery. And Jack himself had discovered this when he was forced to emotionally deal with Laura leaving him in New York and taking Marcus with her.

The cotton crop was now ready for harvesting with a large machine that came as part of the property purchase. The harvested cotton would be sold and processed under an existing contract with a major grower north of Baton Rouge.

Following harvesting, Sam had arranged for soil samples to be taken and tested to ensure that there would be no problems with proposed plantings of other crops due to previous use of chemicals to control weeds and insect pests.

Salina began rejuvenation of the garden where Sam now lived, including the planting of a banana plant which led to much laughter from Sam when he saw it. This required him to provide an explanation to Belinda, who fortunately saw the joke. Further development of Salina's beekeeping project was also proceeding, together with her thoughts about the possibility of establishing a vineyard on part of the newly acquired land. She discussed her growing interest in viticulture with Jack.

"But how much do you know about that? It requires a lot of knowledge in a whole range of areas such as selection of suitable grape varieties, planting, maintenance, winemaking, and marketing," he said.

"Well, I have done some reading, but I must admit my knowledge is not strong just yet."

"Why don't you talk to the Horticulture Centre about enrolling in a viticulture course?"

"Yes. I like that idea. I will phone tomorrow to arrange a meeting."

At the meeting, Salina explained that she was interested in establishing a vineyard at Gratton Grange and would like to undertake a course. She was advised that growing grapes was a challenge in Southern Louisiana due especially to the hot and humid climate that encouraged diseases such as Powdery Mildew, and Pierce's Disease which stunts the growth of the fruit.

However, she was also advised that a lot of research was being undertaken at the Centre to develop grape varieties that are likely to have more resistance to disease in the region. She was told that the Centre would be pleased to enroll her as a student in the two-days-per-week one-year introductory course in viticulture that was about to commence. The course would include lectures and tutorials as well as some hands-on field experience.

That evening, she excitedly informed Jack that she had taken the first step towards establishing a vineyard and that she was confident it would become a profitable part of the new diversified Gratton Grange operations. Along with the citrus trees, other crops, and beekeeping of course.

"My dear, I so admire your enthusiasm. I too believe that we can make this challenging project work."

As the course progressed, Salina eagerly absorbed information. She found the tutorials, with questions and answers, and general discussion with the other students, particularly useful. She had also formed a friendship with Michaela, a twenty-year-old girl in the class whose family owned Banfield Estate, a major well-established winery north of Baton Rouge. The students were taken to inspect the grape vine trials being run by the Horticulture Centre on its small parcel of land just north of New Orleans. They were also invited on a field visit to Banfield Estate to tour the operations and listen to a presentation by Michaela's father Bruce Banfield.

At the official certificate presentation at the end of the course, Salina introduced Jack to Michaela and to Bruce Banfield. They talked about the importance of selecting grape varieties that could tolerate heat and humidity - those that would be the most suitable for the Cranton area. Following the presentation, Salina and Jack met with the head of the Horticulture Centre who suggested a joint arrangement whereby the Center would use some land at Gratton Grange to extend their trial plantings of specially developed grape vine varieties. They would utilize the land at no cost and Gratton Grange would benefit from the provision of expertise and assistance in the establishment of the new vineyard.

The proposal was agreed. It was thought that the main plantings for the new vineyard, apart from the Centre's trial section, would include recently modified red varieties such as Merlot and Cabernet Sauvignon, together with a newly developed hybrid Chardonnay. In addition, a local crisp dry white called Blanc de Bois which had proved successful in some other Louisiana vineyards, including at Banfield Estate further north, would be included. A ten-acre site on slightly undulating well drained land was selected and soil preparation, including ripping and conditioning, was undertaken as well as establishment of an irrigation system.

At a meeting between Jack, Salina, and Sam, the need for effective company governance and procedures was discussed. It was agreed that steps needed to be taken to quickly establish Gratton Grange as an incorporated company. Jack would arrange this with their lawyer in New Orleans. A business plan and budget were also needed, which Jack and Salina would discuss with the family accountant in New Orleans. A specialist wine industry lawyer in Baton Rouge would be consulted about necessary licensing, permits, and taxation requirements for the proposed vineyard.

Gratton Grange Estate would be registered as a business name and the business would become a limited liability company.

Jack was continuing his heavy workload as a surgeon, but the development of Gratton Grange was increasingly taking more of his time. There was a need to provide greater support to Sam and Salina as the enterprise grew. Joey had been doing well as the leading field hand, but it was now time to appoint him assistant manager reporting to Sam, and to promote one of the field hands as leading hand. There was also a need to employ several more field hands to deal with the expanded citrus, vegetable, and other plantings, as well as the proposed vineyard and the growing apiary operation.

Jack asked Sam to look after the new requirements including Joey's enrollment in a part-time agriculture management course. Sam would enroll in a company director's course.

In relation to development of the vineyard, he said: "We need to accept and understand that it will take some time to produce our first vintage and longer to turn a profit for the company, but I am confident that we will give it our best shot and be successful."

Looking at Salina, he added that she would be taking on more responsibility for the effective operation of the expanding apiary as well as a substantial involvement in establishment of the vineyard.

"This greater responsibility should be properly acknowledged," he said.

"Sam, would you please arrange for the conversion of one of the bedrooms at the manor house into an office for Salina."

She was rapidly coming to understand that establishing a vineyard involved much more than knowing how to grow grapes and make wine. Gradually, she had evolved from a jazz singer into a businesswoman. Excited, challenged, and a little apprehensive, she was also buoyed by the strong encouragement and support she knew she could rely on from Jack and Sam.

While Salina's management role was increasing, she was also determined to continue some hands-on work in the fields. One weekend as she tended to the apiary in her protective gear, Jack wandered by and commented that she looked amazing surrounded by the haze generated by the smoke gun she was using. She suggested that he stop 'buzzing around', and instead of making smart remarks, provide some assistance. He quickly retreated to the manor house to watch golf on television.

Later, she entered the house still clad in the protective gear and stood in front of him, blocking the golf. She remained there in a provocative stance as he sat wide-eyed on the couch, oblivious to who had just won the tournament.

Firstly, the head gear came off, which included a frangipani flower that she had picked on the way in, tucked into the side of the facemask. She just stood there looking at him as if refusing to remove the rest. By this stage he could hardly contain his emotions. She slowly lowered the zip down the front of the suit to reveal rather unappealing cotton underwear which she removed and threw to him.

"That's the way I smell after working in the field - it's the sweat of my labor's. Are you impressed?"

He got to his feet, and eager with anticipation, took her in his arms.

"You are very much a multi-talented woman now. Should we celebrate that?"

"I will be disappointed if we don't," she whispered as they sank to the floor.

CHAPTER 13

Planting of the selected grape vine root stock, sourced from a specialist nursery near Baton Rouge, commenced in the first week of March following disking, installation of trellising, and an irrigation system. Care was taken to ensure that spacing between rows was sufficient to enable the easy use of tractors and pickup trucks for activities such as weed control, spraying, and fertilizing. Access for possible future use of harvesting machinery also needed to be provided. In establishing the vineyard, Salina and Sam gained an enormous amount of valuable practical information and guidance through involvement of staff from the Horticulture Centre.

Marcus was now eleven and constantly asking his mother when he could visit Gratton Grange. She finally relented, phoned Jack, and they arranged for the boy to fly to New Orleans for a week during school holidays. For the first time he met his half-sister, Eloise. The timing was good because he was there for her first birthday. A fancy birthday cake with one candle was made by Beth and a small group including Sam and Joey enthusiastically sang happy birthday to the smiling Eloise.

Joey took Marcus under his wing and got him involved in various activities around Gratton Grange including harvesting selected vegetables and some early citrus. He was also introduced to the apiary but was not so keen to get involved there until Joey fitted him with some protective clothing and he ventured closer to inspect the hives. Salina explained the key steps in establishing the vineyard and introduced him to a couple of the staff from the Horticulture Centre who told him about their involvement. Late one afternoon Salina drove him to Sirico's for dinner where they met up with Jack. Marcus sampled Cajan food for the first time and listened to some great jazz and blues music from *The Big Easy Band.*

Prior to the citrus harvest commencing, Jack had asked Sam to investigate possible options for mechanizing the process with a view to improving efficiency, overcoming fluctuating labor availability, and reducing costs. In general, the uptake of mechanical harvesting had been slow in the industry due partly to the damage that could be caused by some forms of the technology. This included the amount of leaves and stems sometimes stripped from the trees by the machinery, which in turn could increase transportation and processing costs compared with hand-harvesting.

Sam also looked at the use of mobile elevating work platforms that could be used for picking the fruit as well as pruning the trees. With this technology the operator stood on the platform and drove the machine along each row. Stopping at each tree, the platform height was adjusted to enable hand picking of the fruit, even at the top of the tree. In his report to Jack, Sam recommended that purchase of a couple of elevating platforms would deliver significant productivity benefits for Gratton Grange. He suggested that this would be an appropriate way to introduce mechanization, but that he should also continue to investigate technological developments relating to the possible introduction of full mechanization.

Initially, one elevating work platform was trialed, which just happened to be while Marcus was staying at Gratton Grange. He was excited to accompany Joey in operating the machine and collecting some lemons, oranges, and limes to place into a picking bag on the platform, which he later proudly showed to Jack and Salina.

"That is a great machine," he told Jack. "You must buy it because it will be really good for harvesting and I would love to drive it next time I am down."

Jack looked at Salina and said: "What a salesman. I am convinced, and I think we should buy two. Do you agree Marcus?"

"Oh yes." And they shook hands on the decision.

Marcus was at an important phase in his education because the subjects he would now start focusing on at high school could have an influence on a later university education. He again told Salina that he wanted to be involved in agriculture when he finished his education. This was then discussed with Jack who was quietly impressed with the way his son was progressing and his growing maturity. Marcus was delighted when Jack undertook to talk to Laura about a preferred educational pathway for him.

When Jack rang, Laura said she was not surprised that Marcus was even more determined to pursue a career in agriculture as he had not stopped talking about it since his return from Gratton Grange. She would arrange to take him to a meeting with the headmaster at his new secondary school. They would map out the way ahead for his education with a focus on appropriate subjects to set him up for later studies relating to agriculture.

Soon after Marcus returned to New York, Jack was having a coffee at the hospital with Tom Eustace when Tom asked him if he and Salina would like to join him and his wife Leanne in a trip to Louisville for the Kentucky Derby. Jack said he would check with Salina, but he was sure they would love to do that.

They flew out of New Orleans in a light aircraft hired by Tom, landed at the Louisville Airport and checked into the Hilton Hotel. That evening they walked to a cute little French restaurant called Le Petite Rendezvous, not far from the Hilton. The atmosphere was joyous rather than raucous, and the cuisine was excellent authentic French. There was an extensive wine list, mainly featuring labels imported from France, but also some from California. This caused Salina to nudge Jack and quietly say: "But no inclusion yet of Louisiana wines. More work must be done to expand our industry's reach into US markets beyond our home state."

Although there was no live music, the piped music had a strong French flavor featuring Edith Piaf as well as Josephine Baker which caused Salina to say to Jack: "What a beautiful little restaurant, it almost feels like we are back in Paris."

This of course led to Tom and Leanne asking about their experiences in the city of romance.

"I think an account of our time in Paris may need some editing," Jack suggested.

"No, tell them everything," Salina exclaimed with a hearty laugh.

Luckily, the waiter suddenly appeared at their table with the main-course dishes which enabled Jack to quickly change the subject to racing in Louisville, rather than racy exploits in Paris.

The city was jumping with visitors from across the US and around the world to attend the famous race. Tom explained that the Kentucky Derby at the Churchill Downs racecourse was first run in 1875 and now headed a two-week festival in the city, attended by the biggest crowd of any race meeting in the US.

"It is a Grade 1 race for three-year-old thoroughbreds over 1.25 miles. Sometimes it is referred to as *The Run for the Roses* because of the blanket of over 500 roses that is traditionally presented to the winner each year," he said.

On arrival at the track, Salina said she had heard that mint julip is the traditional beverage associated with the race and that she would like to try one. They headed to a lounge bar featuring live television coverage of various sports and ordered drinks before sitting down and studying the Derby form guide. Salina and Leanne were quite happy with their mint julips, which the barman had explained consisted of bourbon, mint, and sugar syrup, but Jack and Tom opted for something less exotic and settled on Coors beer.

Around midday they moved outside to a marquee where the lunch menu included Burgoo – a thick stew popular in Kentucky. As they walked into the marquee, Jack thought how stunningly elegant Salina looked in a tailored black suit with a straight pencil-slim skirt, black high heels, and a black Spanish-style brimmed hat that she wore at a slight rakish angle. There was an air of quiet confidence in the way she moved. After looking at the Derby form guide and watching the horses in the mounting yard, she announced that she had decided to put $200 on Alysheba for a win. The horse was a three-year-old bay stallion which Jack pointed out was well fancied by racing experts. It was likely to be at short odds. Salina told him that did not matter – she just liked the look of the horse, that it had a glint in its eye, and there was a friskiness about it.

After the University of Louisville Cardinal Marching Band played *My Old Kentucky Home,* the horses took their places at the starting gates and were soon away to a huge roar from the crowd. Through her binoculars Salina could not identify her selection as the field passed the half-way mark. But as they entered the finishing straight, she yelled: "I can see him, he's moved up through the field and is about sixth, now he's second."

"Oh Jack, he has been nearly knocked to the ground, surely he can't win now."

"But he seems to have recovered, he is battling on, he's running down the leader."

"Jack, I think he may even win."

With a spirited fast finish, Alysheba went to the line to win the 1987 Kentucky Derby by threequarters of a length at odds of US$18.80 for the win. Salina was beside herself with excitement, jumping up and down with joy, flinging her Spanish hat into the air, throwing her arms around Jack, and kissing him repeatedly.

That night they went to a night club one block away from the Hilton where they celebrated the win, had dinner, and danced. Salina impressed Jack with her ability on the dance floor, especially her great sense of rhythm and flexibility. She even encouraged him to try some new moves. Later, on returning from the bathroom, she took Jack aside and told him that she had just had a most interesting experience.

"An attractive lady of about forty years-of-age told me, as I was touching up my make-up in the mirror, that I am beautiful and suddenly kissed me."

Jack stared at her, then said: "Well, you are beautiful, and I don't blame her for having a go."

It became quite a talking point at their table as she told Leanne who quickly asked: "Which woman was it?"

"I don't want to identify her so that we can all look at her. It's not fair to do that," Salina said with a smile.

CHAPTER 14

A few months after the trip to Kentucky, Salina received the shattering news that her father has been seriously injured in a motor accident at a road junction just out of Montgomery. He was in hospital in a coma. Her mother asked her to come home urgently as the prognosis was not good. Jack arranged for a light aircraft to take them to Montgomery where they were met at the airport by Michael and taken to the hospital where Melissa was waiting, looking very downcast.

"Raoul was doing some deliveries in his pickup truck and the other driver did not give way, hitting Raoul's truck on the side at high speed, and causing it to roll several times. Poor Raoul. Now look at the terrible situation we are now facing," an anguished Melissa said.

Soon after, a doctor entered the room and explained the outlook. He said a decision would need to be made the following day as to whether the life-support system should be turned off. Scans had revealed significant brain damage and the patient so far was not showing any positive signs.

Salina kissed her father on the forehead and burst into tears. She felt like she was living in a dream and could not believe the tragedy that she was now witnessing, and how easily the life of a good man could be destroyed at just 62.

As they left the hospital Jack suggested they get some Chinese take-away for dinner and a couple of bottles of wine, try to relax a little, and discuss how to deal with the situation they now faced. Over dinner he commented that it appeared highly likely that Raoul's condition would not improve and that they must prepare for the worst. Melissa said decisions needed to be made about the future of the business which had grown significantly over recent years and was now quite prosperous. She looked at Michael, who was now thirty, and asked whether he was prepared to take over his father's role as managing director of the family business.

Michael was very quick and clear in his response.

"It would be a great honor to step into my father's role in the company. Having worked beside him for several years I now have a strong knowledge of the business and a vision of the way ahead to ensure its continuing success," he said.

"I am so pleased Michael. Your father would want you to take over. That was always our plan," said his mother wistfully.

The next day the family again met with the doctor, plus a specialist neurological physician. It was agreed to remove life-support from Raoul.

In planning the funeral service, the family agreed that Michael would say a few words at the beginning. Salina said she would be too emotional to speak but offered to sing a gospel song with the choir and involve the entire congregation as the casket left the church. Melissa asked Jack if he would deliver the main eulogy about the life of Raoul.

At the funeral service in a large old Baptist Church in Montgomery, a huge congregation of mostly black mourners had gathered to pay their last respects to Raoul. Michael was the first to speak. He said what a wonderful family man his father had been. How he had struggled to ensure that his children were raised with a good education and strong ethics. And how much his father had loved their mother.

Then Jack strode to the front and, with Salina standing beside him, in an action designed to startle the congregation, he thumped the pulpit and said:

"Raoul was a good man. He loved this country, loved Montgomery, and most of all he loved his family. He did not deserve to die in this way. Although many here today had known him a lot longer than me, I quickly grew to admire him enormously. He was an honest, hard-working man of strong convictions. I am lucky to be the husband of his beautiful daughter Salina, who is standing beside me, and proud to be a member of Raoul's family.

"He was the product of a long line of disadvantaged African Americans, starting with his ancestors being transported to Montgomery and sold into slavery. Even after the Civil War, life continued to be extremely challenging for black communities as they suffered discrimination and often blatant racism.

"As many of you will know, in the fifties and sixties this city of Montgomery was the center of the civil rights movement and Raoul attended some major historical events with his father. It helped to shape much of his future determination to build a happy and successful life. In 1955 Rosa Parkes was arrested for refusing to give up her seat to a white man which sparked the Montgomery bus boycott, led by Martin Luther King Jr. A judge later ruled that Montgomery's bus segregation was unconstitutional and the buses were desegregated.

"In 1965 Raoul, at 40 years of age, took part with his father when some 25,000 marched in Montgomery calling for voting rights which led to the Voting Rights Act of 1965 and enforced the rights of African Americans and other minorities to vote. Thankfully, things have changed significantly from those dreadful dark days that Raoul's forebears endured.

"Raoul saw education as an essential pathway to success and completed a business management degree at Alabama State University. He carried his belief in education over to the development of his children. Michael later completed the same course at ASU and while at high school in Montgomery, Salina undertook music, singing and dance classes.

"We are here today to pay tribute and give thanks to a man of principle who has given so much to this city of Montgomery over many years. An intelligent, hard-working, kind and thoughtful man that we are lucky to have known."

At the end of the service, Salina stood beside the organist, flanked by two female violinists and, inviting the choir and congregation to join her, began singing the stirring gospel song *Swing Low Sweet Chariot.* She felt that Raoul would have wanted an uplifting song, not a dirge. As she sang, she raised her hands towards the bare rafters in the high cathedral ceiling of the church, dropped her hands, and then raised them again as if to seek a response from the heavens. The congregation stood as one and burst into a glorious high-volume rendition of the song's chorus *Coming for To Carry Me Home.*

The next day the Montgomery Mercury carried a full-page feature on Raoul and his funeral. There was also extensive coverage on local television and radio as well as on national evening news. Salina and Jack stayed on for a few days in Montgomery to support Melissa in her grief and then flew back to New Orleans. In the plane, it was obvious that Salina was having difficulty dealing with her father's passing and Jack suggested that they should take a holiday. She brightened at this suggestion and said: "I have always wanted to go to LA and also to Santa Monica and ride on that big Ferris Wheel at the pier - we can use the money that I won at the Kentucky Derby."

Arriving home, they advised Sam that they would be flying to California the next weekend with Eloise and taking Beth with them. Reservations were made for a week's stay at the luxury Santa Monica Beach Resort. Julian at the clinic and Tom at the hospital both strongly supported the planned holiday.

Beth, who had only been to California once before, many years ago, was excited about the forthcoming trip. Salina and Jack smiled as they heard her telling Eloise about how they would be flying on a big bird across the country to a lovely warm place with beautiful beaches where they could go for a swim and ride on a big Ferris Wheel.

CHAPTER 15

On arrival in Los Angeles, Jack rented a Chevrolet SUV and after piling in their luggage they drove the short distance to Santa Monica and checked into the resort on Ocean Avenue. Their spacious two-bedroom suite was on the top floor overlooking the beach. It included a large family room with access to a sunny balcony, and a fully equipped kitchen.

They woke on the first morning to light misty rain which quickly cleared to a bright sunny day with a clear blue sky. The extensive buffet breakfast was in a ground floor dining room where a young waitress arranged a highchair for the smiling Eloise. Over breakfast they made plans for the week ahead including a trip to Santa Catalina Island, plus visiting Disneyland, and Sunset Strip. A visit to Rodeo Drive to satisfy Salina's wish for some upmarket shopping was also included. On their way to breakfast the concierge had advised that they should visit the farmers market on Main Street in Santa Monica for whatever provisions they might need for their kitchen.

After settling Eloise into the lightweight baby stroller brought from Gratton Grange, they set out on the easy walk to the farmer's market. The market, which stretched down both sides of Main Street, was famous in the region for its huge range of high-quality fresh vegetables and fruit, and the friendly knowledgeable stall holders. There was a great atmosphere enhanced by several street musicians and singers.

Salina declared: "This is my type of farmers market."

The happy foursome browsed the array of produce on offer and filled two shopping bags, that they bought on entering the market, with enough produce to provide for some dinners and lunches. Then they bought ice-creams, with a special strawberry one for Eloise, and chatted to some of the locals about their plans for the next few days.

Back at the resort Beth made some chicken and avocado sandwiches for lunch. It was then time for a walk on the beach, a paddle in the shallows of the Pacific Ocean, a stroll on the pier, and a ride on the Ferris Wheel.

The sand squeaked between their toes as they walked on Santa Monica beach. Jack commented that unlike the pebble-beaches found in many parts of Europe, this beach was especially visitor friendly. With its wide and long expanse, it continued for miles through other famous beaches including Muscle Beach, Venice Beach and Marina Del Rey.

Eloise was wide-eyed as her father took her to the edge of the water and then squealed with excitement as a small wave came in and wet the bottom of her shorts. They walked along to the pier where a range of vendors offered snacks and jewelry for sale and where an artist sketched visitors. Salina sat on a chair with Eloise on her knee and asked him to sketch them with the beach in the background.

Then it was time to board the Ferris Wheel. First aboard was Beth with Eloise followed by Salina and Jack in a capsule behind them. The wheel turned slowly as they moved to some 130 feet above the Santa Monica pier. Eloise clung tightly to Beth's hand while Salina behind held hands with Jack and took in the panoramic view of the Southern California coastline.

On the way back to the resort they bought some fresh fish from a vendor near the pier and Beth said she would make a garden salad with produce purchased earlier at the farmer's market.

The next day they drove in the SUV to Disneyland in Anaheim, stopping first at Knott's Berry Farm which was reputed to have the biggest and juiciest strawberries in the world. Eloise loved strawberry flavor and her face was soon smeared with the red juice. This was a huge day out for the little girl who wore a pretty floral dress and was in high spirits as they entered Disneyland. She was introduced to Mickey Mouse and his friend Minnie as well as Donald Duck and his friend Daffy. Mickey asked if she was having a nice time in California to which she shyly nodded, and he took her by the hand to receive a giant serving of pink fairy floss which was almost as big as Eloise. They then visited some of the attractions including the hall of mirrors and went on the caves tunnel boat ride where all sorts of fictional figures, such as witches, wizards and pirates emerged as they went along. Eloise went from being scared and screaming to being happy and clapping. She was exhausted and fell asleep as they drove back to Santa Monica.

The early morning high-speed catamaran from Long Beach took about one hour to reach the town of Avalon on Santa Catalina Island. A guide on board told the passengers that the island was first inhabited by Indigenous American Indians before Avalon was established in the late 1800's. He said that now this fascinating island had only about 800 cars and trucks, 1,000 golf carts, just 3,000 permanent residents, and around one million visitors each year.

"The island, with a total area of 76 square miles, is 21 miles long and 8 miles wide and has many canyons and ridges where wild buffalo roam, steep cliffs to the sea, and rocky beaches."

The guide added that Santa Catalina had long been a playground for the rich and famous, including Hollywood film stars. "In 1981 the island received world-wide publicity about the disappearance one night of film star Natalie Wood off a yacht moored in Avalon harbor owned by Natalie and her husband, film star Robert Wagner. Apart from drowning, many of the circumstances are unknown. It was never determined how she entered the water, although Wagner was named as a person of interest in the investigation," he said.

Jack, Salina, Beth, and Eloise had a late breakfast at a café on the waterfront. They then visited some of Avalon's points of interest including the casino and the local museum before hiring a golf buggy to explore further around the town and a little into the hinterland. Mid-afternoon they caught the catamaran back to Long Beach, collected the SUV, and returned to Santa Monica.

Salina mentioned that the following day she would like to visit Sunset Strip and do some shopping on Rodeo Drive. Jack interrupted and said he always wanted to have a drink at the Chateau Marmont. He told her that it is high up at one end of Sunset Boulevard - they could have lunch there and then go on to Sunset Strip and Rodeo Drive. This suggestion was met with an enthusiastic response from Salina and an offer from Beth to look after Eloise for the day.

"Jack, I would like to wear my new cowboy hat. Would that be OK?"

"Sure, you look stunning in that, but maybe save it for Sunset Strip. The Chateau may not let you in."

The traffic was heavy as they drove from Santa Monica down Wilshire Boulevard to Sunset Boulevard in Hollywood. Jack explained that the Chateau

Marmont was modelled somewhat on the Chateau d' Ambroise in France's Loire Valley. It had 63 rooms including suites, cottages, and bungalows, many with private terraces and spectacular views. Over the years its celebrity guests included Greta Garbo, Rudolph Valentino, Bertolt Brecht, F Scott Fitzgerald, Billy Wilder, and Howard Hughes. Errol Flynn was a regular who is believed to have bedded his three wives there in rather quick succession. But it was not all gaiety and raucous partying. In 1982 John Belushi took a fatal drug overdose at the Chateau.

As they entered the hotel Salina commented about the strong imposing architecture.

"There is something forbidding about this place, and even a sense of the salacious and scandalous."

"You are on the ball there. It also has a well-deserved reputation for debauchery, and is said to be populated by people on the way up or on the way down. Some time ago I read a magazine article about this hotel and its history and thought it would be interesting to visit."

"OK, let's go. I am game, and hungry. But I reckon I could wear my cowboy hat here, although I will not, as I suspect it would make you uncomfortable."

"Thank you my dear."

They walked through the hotel's dark gothic-influence lobby to the leafy garden terrace where a waiter seated them at a table next to a large potted palm. Two glasses of Californian Sauvignon Blanc, a Waldorf salad for Salina and a Caesar salad for Jack, plus a seafood platter for two were ordered.

Further down the terrace there was a white middle eastern desert-style tent with an open front which attracted Salina's attention. About ten people, seated inside on large cushions around a low central table, were having a very chatty and happy lunch.

"Isn't that Johnny Depp next to that gorgeous blond?" she whispered.

"Yes, I think you are right. I'm trying not to stare."

"Me too."

CHAPTER 16

As they left for a stroll down Sunset Strip, Salina, now in her cowboy hat, said she was glad Jack had suggested lunch at the Chateau and was fascinated by its somewhat scandalous history.

"Maybe it's just as well that we visited for lunch, rather than drinks at night. I also enjoyed our visit to the risqué Folies Bergère in Paris which you also suggested."

"Excuse me, but it was your aunt Claudette who suggested we go there. But I must say it was an excellent suggestion."

Jack commented that during the roaring 1920's Sunset Strip was famous as a hangout for gangsters as well as film stars, but in more recent times it had become well known for its music, entertainment and extensive dining and shopping options.

"Here is the Viper Room which was a mobster gambling den in the 1940's. It is now a nightclub frequented by film stars. Over there is the Rainbow Bar & Grill where Marilyn Monroe and baseball great Joe DiMaggio met on a blind date in 1952. John Belushi ate his last meal there not long before overdosing at his Chateau Marmont bungalow."

"Gee Jack, we have just left the Chateau which has been, and maybe still is, a hotbed of debauchery and now we are strolling through an area where gangsters ran a number of operations, and where other scandalous activities apparently occurred. I don't know whether to be excited or concerned about what might be around the next corner."

"Well, this is another view of life which is certainly a lot different to the life we lead at Gratton Grange, across the other side of the country. I think it's time we headed to the more serene atmosphere of Rodeo Drive."

Arriving in the center of Rodeo Drive, they found a nice café where Jack could order a coffee and read the Los Angeles Times. Salina took off with a bounce in her step; an indication that a serious shopping expedition was about to commence.

She strolled along the prime luxury shopping section of the street located north of Wilshire Boulevard and south of Little Santa Monica Boulevard, entered the Beverly Wilshire Hotel for a quick look around, and then browsed through the offerings of various high-end fashion shops.

Nearly two hours later she rejoined Jack at the café. An excited Salina displayed her purchases including two dresses, a pair of slacks, a jacket, and a pair of sandals, plus a nice top as a present for Beth. She then drew another parcel from a bag and handed it to Jack with a kiss. It was a superb Ralph Lauren dark brown soft leather bomber-style jacket that she demanded he immediately try on.

"Oh, that color really suits you and makes you look even more handsome Dr Lansell."

"What a gorgeous thoughtful lady you are. Thank you so much, I love it."

"Don't thank me darling, thank *Alysheba* for winning the Kentucky Derby."

On their last day in Santa Monica, they had a late breakfast at the resort and then, at Eloise's insistence, went to the beach for a couple of hours under a large multi-colored umbrella. She had kept sending messages by repeating 'beach' and pointing in that direction from her seat on the balcony. Beth had earlier bought her a small bucket and spade and Jack showed her how to make a sandcastle, complete with a functional moat, courtesy of the incoming tide.

On the way back to the resort they passed an attractive restaurant called Seascape located near the pier. At their suite, Beth suggested that Jack and Salina should have dinner together at Seascape as it was the last night of their holiday, and she would look after Eloise.

For dinner, Salina decided to wear the bright yellow mini-dress she had bought in Rodeo Drive, teamed with leather sandals, while Jack chose a red polo shirt, beige slacks, and slip-on canvas loafers. As they strolled along the beach, he told Salina that he had spoken to the concierge at their resort about Seascape and was informed that it was an excellent long-established restaurant that had retained its elegant beachfront atmosphere from an earlier period in Santa Monica's history.

They walked into the main lounge with its sweeping ocean views, exquisite velvet drapes and elegant period furnishings. There was a pianist at a grand piano playing classical compositions including, Salina noted, Haydn.

"Joseph Haydn is my favorite classical composer. He is generally regarded as the father of symphony, and the string quartet, with his superbly light and elegant compositions. It is not surprising that he had a significant influence on the work of Mozart and Beethoven."

"I do not know a lot about Haydn, but I remember that my piano teacher in Washington was a big admirer of his compositions," said Jack.

Looking around, Salina commented that the room had a lovely, refined atmosphere: "We should have a drink here before moving into the dining area for dinner."

"What a good idea, why don't you go to that little table at the window. I will get drinks from the bar over there."

They took in the magnificent ocean views stretching out before them across to the nearby pier, and then looked around the room. It was occupied mainly by couples of various ages in obviously expensive smart casual attire. The low hum of conversations pervaded the room; some in foreign languages.

"There is a serenity here, like the whole world could be at peace, which of course unfortunately it is not," observed Salina.

Ocean views again greeted them from their dining table. A friendly waiter soon approached and explained the menu in detail. The restaurant, which was packed, had a more casual beachy feel compared with the more upmarket atmosphere of the adjacent lounge area. They both ordered seared scallops and a large garden salad to share, together with a bottle of Santa Barbara Chardonnay.

As they finished a delicious ricotta cheesecake with cherry compote, Jack commented on a table nearby.

"Look at that couple over there Salina. They both look extremely bored and have not spoken to each other for quite some time. How sad. There is really not much point in being together."

"Thankfully Jack, there is no way that will ever happen with us. We enjoy each other's company too much, chatting about all sorts of things. Maybe their life has become empty and lacks purpose for some reason. It makes one appreciate even more how lucky we are to have met each other and the benefits and challenges that our diverse lives present – you with your medical profession and me helping to develop a successful Gratton Grange. There is never a boring moment because there is always something to discuss and plans to make."

CHAPTER 17

A rriving back at Gratton Grange from Los Angeles, Salina rang her mother and spoke to Michael who told her that Melissa seemed to be coping reasonably well. She was spending a couple of hours each day serving at the hardware store, which helped to take her mind off the sudden loss of Raoul.

Jack returned to work at the clinic and, in a meeting with Julian, put forward a proposal to redefine and expand its operations.

"We are both specialists in reconstructive surgery as well as undertaking some general surgery. During patient recovery from surgery, I believe there is an obvious need for specialist care that is sometimes not being met, or at least not always met effectively. We are often dealing with extremely traumatic injuries which we do our best to repair and restore function as close as possible to normal. Full recovery can sometimes be a long and challenging road for the patient, so professional specialist assistance can be crucial, especially in areas such as clinical psychology and physiotherapy. Traumatic injuries can lead to conditions such as anxiety and depression that require early professional intervention.

"I am proposing that we invite a clinical psychologist and a physiotherapist to join our clinic to provide a whole-of-service offering that commences, where necessary, soon after surgery. There is an obvious strong link between the type of surgery we specialize in and ensuring the best possible recovery for our patients. My proposal will enable us as surgeons to ensure that we are involved in the entire recovery process."

"Jack, I really like this exciting new initiative for our clinic. How do we go about recruiting?"

"Why don't we talk to Tom at the hospital?"

At their meeting, Tom was supportive of the proposal. He suggested they approach Dr Rebecca Durham, a clinical psychologist who had worked on secondment at the hospital in New Orleans following the hurricane disaster. She was now back at a hospital in New Haven, Connecticut. He also said he had heard good reports about Gavin, a physiotherapist who worked at a hospital in Baton Rouge and who might be interested in joining a private clinic.

Straight after the meeting Jack phoned Rebecca and then Gavin. Rebecca was quite interested in the proposal and asked Jack to send her a written offer which she could discuss with her partner Darren who was a journalist on a local newspaper in New Haven.

After speaking briefly to Gavin, it was agreed that he would visit the clinic for an interview with Jack and Julian. Jack then told Tom at the hospital that Rebecca was interested but was concerned about obtaining employment in New Orleans for her partner.

"Over recent years I have got to know the editor of the New Orleans Gazette quite well. Let me talk to him about whether he has a vacancy for a journalist," said Tom.

He soon got back to Jack with the news that the editor would be interested in meeting Darren and suggested that maybe he and Rebecca could fly down from New Haven to discuss a possible move to New Orleans. This proposal was received by Rebecca with enthusiasm and arrangements were made for them to visit the following week.

Rebecca visited the clinic and then caught up with Tom at the hospital, while Darren went to an interview at the newspaper. Later, they met with broad smiles at Sirico's for lunch with Julian and Jack.

"How did things go?" asked Jack, already observing that they both appeared to be in a happy mood.

"Darren has been offered a job at the Gazette," said Rebecca. "The editor was impressed in his broad reporting experience in New Haven and the interesting colorful style of writing that he could bring to the Gazette. In relation to me personally, I am impressed with the plans that you have for the clinic and the important role that I could play as a partner. I have noticed the impressive recovery this city has achieved since I was here immediately after the hurricane. The vibrant atmosphere of the city has returned. Darren and I agree that we would be able to make a useful contribution to the city's progress, and we would very much like to move here to live and work."

The following day at a meeting with Jack and Julian, Gavin accepted an offer of employment as the clinic's physiotherapist with a salary package that included accommodation in the apartment above the clinic that was now owned by the business.

CHAPTER 18

Almost five years after the initial vineyard plantings it was now time for the first harvest at Gratton Grange Estate. Salina and Jack visited Banfield Estate to talk to Bruce and Michaela about the possibility of them processing the grapes from Gratton Grange. They received a friendly welcome, a mutually beneficial agreement was reached, and a contract signed. On the way back they met with a graphic designer in Baton Rouge that Bruce had recommended. The design of Gratton Grange Estate labels was discussed for the bottling of their red and white vintages at Banfield Estate.

Following the initial plantings, the vineyard had been extended and now covered 20 acres, with plans being developed to at least double the existing acreage. Positive reviews of the first harvest offerings from the initial plantings flowed from wine experts and, much to Salina's delight, good coverage was received in the local media. The Cranton Chronicle ran a full-page feature with a photo of her and Sam amongst the vines, glasses of wine in hand as they sampled the results of their labors. Good coverage was also achieved in the New Orleans Gazette.

In addition, Salina had been putting a lot of effort into development of the apiary. The number of hives had tripled, and she had arranged for the registration of Gratton Grange Honey as a trademark and trading name.

Attractive product packaging had been designed. She and Sam had prepared an aggressive marketing plan, especially involving supermarkets in New Orleans, Baton Rouge, Natchez and Cranton, plus Mobile and Montgomery in Alabama. The marketing plan included editorial coverage and advertising in local media in each town. Sales were steadily increasing, particularly in Montgomery, where she had appointed her mother Melissa as distribution manager. A key thrust of the promotional efforts was a focus on the health benefits of honey.

At a board meeting, Jack reported that Gratton Grange was showing a good profit for the year. The apiary was providing a useful and growing contribution, and the vineyard was displaying excellent prospects of making a substantial contribution to the company's bottom line. He also announced that Salina, as a past student, had been invited to give a talk to the current class at the Horticulture Centre about her experiences in establishing the vineyard at Gratton Grange Estate. She was honored to be invited do the presentation, but very anxious at suddenly being recognized for her efforts in dealing with the challenges and assisting to progress the wine industry in Louisiana. Jack told her that she had to have faith in her abilities and that it was a great opportunity to further promote Gratton Grange Estate as well as the Centre.

"As a surgeon, every day I need to have faith in my abilities and it's not always easy. I will help you prepare some notes. You will be fine once you start speaking," he reassured her.

With Jack, Sam and Joey sitting at the back of the lecture room, Salina presented her address like a professional and received warm acclaim at the conclusion. The Centre had also arranged for her address to be filmed so that it could be shown to future students attending the same course.

At the next board meeting it was agreed that a restaurant, wine tasting room and a car park should be built near the manor house on the driveway that led to the jetty. It was also decided that Jack would instruct the same architect who had designed the manor house to ensure that the styles of the two buildings complimented each other. Salina said she would like to design the interior look of the new building and select the interior furnishings. She also suggested that they should consider appointing her friend Jessica, who was currently head waitress at Sirico's, to manage the new enterprise. These suggestions were agreed on the proviso that Jessica attend a short course on business management in New Orleans which Gratton Grange Estate would pay for, and that she would report directly to Sam.

Rapid progress was made in constructing the single-story restaurant and tasting room. Salina wanted a warm natural look in the design of the interiors which featured a lot of exposed timber beams as well as walls of exposed brickwork, an open fireplace for colder nights, and burnt-orange-colored polished concrete floors providing easy access from the tasting room to the adjoining restaurant. As well as indoor dining, the restaurant would offer outdoor dining under big market umbrellas on a large deck over-looking the Mississippi River. A pathway under an extended vine-covered pergola was planned to lead to the entrance of the restaurant from the main driveway where Salina would establish garden beds to provide a blaze of brightly colored flowers.

A full-color brochure with photographs was prepared to promote the Gratton Grange Estate restaurant, which would offer fine cuisine with a French influence utilizing fresh vegetables, herbs and fruit grown on the Estate. An authentic paddock-to-plate dining experience would be provided. The restaurant would be able to seat up to 150 people, so functions such as weddings and birthday gatherings would be promoted as well as commercial events including seminars, training courses and corporate product launches.

The first function booked was an engagement party with 80 guests for a couple from New Orleans who knew Salina from regularly dining at Sirico's. They were so pleased with the experience at the Gratton Grange Estate restaurant that they also wanted to book for their wedding celebrations, but on the proviso that Salina would sing. She agreed to sing two songs at the wedding for which she would not charge a fee.

Bookings quickly escalated as word of the new high-quality restaurant spread and it was soon booked out one month ahead. As well as bottle sales at the tasting room, an associated side business selling citrus fruit, berries, pecans, herbs, relishes, and of course honey, to the guests as they departed the restaurant, also began to take off.

Tourists from around the world often arrived aboard the Mississippi Princess. Bernard would announce passengers arriving at the jetty and departing by blowing the paddle steamer's whistle.

CHAPTER 19

After the Gratton Grange Estate restaurant had been trading for about twelve months a dramatic event occurred. It was around 3.00 PM and luckily most of the customers had finished lunch and departed. An obviously drug-affected male entered the restaurant and held a handgun to the ribs of a gentleman who was in the process of paying his bill, demanding his credit card and wallet. He then screamed at Jessica to give him the contents of the till, which she did without hesitation, nervously exclaiming: "Oh Gerry".

On the way out he grabbed a bottle of wine, ran to a stolen pickup truck, took off in a cloud of dust down the driveway and headed north towards Baton Rouge. Jessica immediately phoned the police in New Orleans who told her a car and helicopter were on the way. She then phoned Salina who raced across from the manor house.

A police patrol car from Cranton arrived plus a special forces police helicopter from New Orleans. The helicopter landed in the carpark of the restaurant and the police team leader spoke briefly to Jessica before radioing ahead to police in Baton Rouge and then taking off at a rapid pace in pursuit of the fugitive. Police in the car from Cranton stayed to talk to Jessica and Salina.

With the helicopter in constant communication with police on the ground, a roadblock was setup on the main road to Baton Rouge. About twenty miles north of Gratton Grange, the fugitive pulled into a service station to refuel using the stolen credit card. Just as he was about to leave, the helicopter arrived which caused the fugitive to draw his gun and force the service station attendant to lock the door. He then ordered him and an elderly retired couple from Cranton into the storeroom before taking up position behind the main counter. A police officer with a loud hailer ordered him to come out unarmed with his hands in the air but there was no response. The leader of the helicopter unit rang the service station phone which was answered by the fugitive and a lengthy negotiation took place. With the fugitive still refusing to come out, the leader ordered a window to be broken and tear gas capsules to be fired inside. Over the loud hailer he told the fugitive that he had one minute to throw his gun through the broken window and to come out with his hands in the air, otherwise they would break in and remove him.

Soon after, the gun was flung from the window, the door opened, and the fugitive appeared. He was quickly cuffed, taken into custody, and the much-relieved hostages were released from the storeroom. By now the car park was crowded with media including TV crews filming the scene and interviewing the service center attendant, the hostages, and the police commander.

Sam, Belinda, and Joey had arrived at the manor house shortly after the drama at the restaurant. After comforting Jessica, Beth had prepared a large platter of biscuits, cheeses, olives, strawberries, and blueberries. They were much relieved when watching the early evening news to learn that the fugitive had been captured. Jessica was still shaken by the ordeal. She explained that she and Gerry, who was a motor mechanic in New Orleans, had a brief relationship some six months earlier which she had terminated due to his sometimes aggressive, demanding, and erratic attitude.

"I could not believe my eyes when he walked in with that gun. I was stunned," she said.

"I had found him to be difficult to deal with and discovered that he had a significant drug problem. But I certainly did not expect this. Increasingly his moods would shift from one extreme to another. Maybe what happened at the restaurant was his way of getting back at me for ending our relationship."

After taking a statement from Jessica, the police filed a report in New Orleans. Several days later, she received a request to visit the central police station to be interviewed about elements of her statement and her relationship with Gerry.

With Salina by her side, she entered the station and was met by Peter Mahony, a young detective who showed them to a sparsely furnished interview room. He emphasized that the interview was just a routine follow-up to the statement she had already provided to the police.

"Jessica, I am interested to know about your relationship with Gerry Coleman. How long have you known him?"

"About six months."

"Where did you meet him?"

"At the workshop where I took my car for servicing."

"Did you go out with him regularly after that?"

"No, we only went out about three or four times. He had a problem with drugs which resulted in quite severe mood swings, so I broke off the relationship."

"You never lived with him?"

"No."

"Were you surprised that he committed armed robbery at the restaurant that you manage at Gratton Grange Estate?"

"I knew that his drug-taking could cause him to be mentally unstable, but I certainly did not expect him to confront me like he did and carry out an armed robbery. It was a terrifying experience."

Turning to Salina as Jessica's employer, Mahony asked how long she has known Jessica.

"I first met her several years ago when we both worked at Sirico's and decided to share an apartment nearby. I hope you are not suggesting by all your questions that there may have been some type of collusion between Jessica and Gerry in relation to the armed robbery."

"As I said at the outset, this is merely a routine interview following a particularly serious crime. The customer who was forced to handover his credit card and wallet has said in a statement that Jessica referred to Gerry by name during the holdup. Therefore, I am simply following up as to how she knew him and any relationship that they had."

"I just want to point out that she phoned the police and reported the crime as soon as Gerry left the restaurant, even before she contacted me. I have the highest regard for Jessica's integrity and loyalty, both as an employee and close friend," Salina said politely but firmly.

"OK ladies, that will be all. Thank you for attending today and for your cooperation in the interview. Charges are likely to be laid soon against Gerry and we understand that he intends to plead guilty which would mean an expeditious process through the court."

Driving back to Gratton Grange Jessica looked at Salina and said: "How lucky I am to have a friend like you when confronted with such a challenging situation."

"That's what real friends are for in times of such need. I'm sure you would have done the same for me."

A few weeks later Gerry came before the court charged with armed robbery, unlawful detainment, resisting arrest, possession of drugs and driving a stolen vehicle under the influence of drugs. He was sentenced to seven years jail with a minimum of five before being eligible for parole.

CHAPTER 20

Following the purchase of Cooper's property, most of the acreage that he had planted with cotton was now utilized to extend the Gratton Grange citrus plantings. This increased volume led to Jack and Sam again discussing greater use of mechanization in harvesting. It was decided that Sam would visit the suppliers of citrus harvesting machines in Florida and talk to the managers of a couple of large citrus plantations about the benefits and latest developments in mechanized harvesting.

In Florida, Sam found that many of the issues that had slowed the uptake of mechanized citrus harvesting had been addressed and largely overcome. Damage to the fruit and the citrus trees had been significantly reduced as well as the amount of debris mixed with the collected fruit.

It had been estimated that harvesting accounted for up to 50 percent of the total cost of producing citrus, so it was important to develop effective cost reduction technologies, especially when dealing with increasing competition in a global market. The growers that Sam spoke to were now committed to mechanical harvesting and saw it as necessary, especially on large acreages, to ensure future viability. It was suggested that he consider trialing a mechanical harvester on a lease basis and was given a contact at a machinery agent in New Orleans to talk to.

On returning to Gratton Grange, Sam reported his findings to Jack. It was agreed that he discuss a leasing arrangement with the agricultural machinery agent in New Orleans. Maybe a large mechanical harvester could be used for the bulk of the citrus crops while the existing mobile elevating work platforms could be used to hand-pick fruit destined for the table to ensure the highest possible quality for that market.

In negotiations, it was agreed with the agent that a newly released mechanical harvester developed in Florida would be provided on lease at a reduced rate for the upcoming citrus harvest at Gratton Grange. An experienced technician and operator provided by the agent would train an operator provided by Sam. He would also be available on call to deal with any issues during the harvest. Gratton Grange could return the machine to the agent at the end of the harvest or, if happy with the machine's performance, purchase the machine at an agreed discount price.

Apart from one or two minor issues that were quickly rectified, Sam was impressed with how quickly the harvest was completed compared with previous years. Only minor damage occurred to the fruit or trees and the amount of debris mixed with the harvested fruit was minimal. The agent suggested that if Gratton Grange was prepared to publicly endorse the benefits of the machine, then an even better purchase price could be offered.

"Jack, maybe we should consider purchasing the machine at a significantly discounted price. It would be a substantial capital outlay, but the machine would then be available to us whenever required. We could also hire it out to other citrus growers in Louisiana, and even those in neighboring states," said an enthusiastic Sam.

"OK Sam, I will call a board meeting, explain the perceived benefits, and seek agreement to proceed. Maybe we could also use Cooper's old cotton harvesting machine, which is gathering dust in the shed, as a trade-in."

After discussing the proposal with the company's accountant in New Orleans, Sam prepared a paper for consideration at an urgently called board meeting which the accountant also attended. Following considerable discussion, the proposal was approved. Gratton Grange was indeed about to become an even more efficient operation in line with Jack's original plan.

After a few days leave, during which she stayed with friends in Baton Rouge while Salina managed the restaurant, Jessica returned to work feeling rejuvenated. Business had initially slowed after the robbery but quickly returned to its normal hectic pace.

Two years after establishment, Salina received advice that the restaurant had been nominated for Southern Louisiana Restaurant of the Year by the New Orleans Chamber of Commerce. The winner would soon be announced at a gala event at the town hall.

Over 200 guests gathered for dinner and a series of award presentations in a range of business categories. Salina had organized a table that included Jack,

Eloise, Sam and his partner Belinda, Jessica, and Joey. An excited Eloise, who was now eight, could not sit still and wandered around the room talking to various people, most of whom she had never met before.

After the main course, the mayor of New Orleans welcomed and thanked all the guests for their attendance at what she referred to as a most important annual occasion in the business and social life of the city. Official winners in each category were then progressively announced and presentations made. About half-way through, the mayor announced Gratton Grange Estate as Restaurant of the Year. Eloise, who was chatting with new friends at a table near the back of the room, clapped enthusiastically and announced: "That's my mom." before scampering back to hug her father.

The mayor, with Salina and Jessica now standing beside her, turned to them, and said:

"Through the development of Gratton Grange and establishment of the restaurant, you have helped to open up Louisiana to the world and promote the fruits of our labors in this state. Tourism has doubled in the past decade, and we have now developed into a thriving economy after recovering from the hurricane disaster. You very much deserve this award and the congratulations of us all."

She then asked the manager of Sirico's, which had won the award the previous year, to come forward and make the trophy presentation. Now it was his turn to present the award to two former employees of his restaurant – it was a moment that made him feel immensely proud. Salina commented on what an honor it was to receive the award. She paid tribute to the dedicated contribution made by Jessica as manager of the restaurant, where the trophy would be prominently displayed.

Sitting watching the presentation, Sam could not help reflecting on the enormous progress that Gratton Grange had made and his part in it since the dark days of the hurricane. He was almost overcome with pride and emotion as he shook hands with Jack and hugged Salina and Jessica. Sirico's *Big Easy Band* played as Lenny, a local African American with a wonderful rich deep baritone voice, sang *Old Man River,* and people enjoyed the finest of Louisiana food and wine.

Before launching into the song, Lenny told the audience that the music was by Jerome Kern with lyrics by Oscar Hammerstein II. He said the song featured in the 1927 musical *Show Boat* and became world famous when sung by Paul Robeson in the classic 1936 film version of the musical.

He explained that it contrasts the struggles and hardships of African Americans with the endless flow of the Mississippi:

> *Ol' man river*
> *That ol' man river*
> *He don't say nothing*
> *But he must know something*
> *Cause he just keeps rolling*
> *He keeps rolling along*
>
> *Rollin' along*
> *He don't plant tators*
> *He don't plant cotton*
> *Them that plants 'em is soon forgotten*
> *But ol' man river*
> *He keeps rolling along.*

Arriving back at Gratton Grange, Jack and Salina noticed Jessica's SUV parked at Joey's house.

"That's interesting," she said.

"Very. Could be the start of a whole new coupling at Gratton Grange."

The following day Jessica mentioned to Salina that she had stayed the night at Joey's and asked about his background.

"He was a young field hand with Sam at the time that Jack bought Sam's property after the hurricane and named it Gratton Grange. I do not know much about his family background except that they live somewhere in New Orleans. But I must say that he has proved to be a good and loyal employee."

"Thanks Salina. He seems to be a nice but rather private guy. I would like to get to know him better."

CHAPTER 21

Jessica lived in a small unit attached to the restaurant and Joey began having the occasional meal there and staying the night. Or they would walk to his house after she finished work and stay the night there. One evening they were sitting on his veranda drinking coffee when he told her he loved her and asked her to move in and live with him.

"Joey, it would be nice if I had a good, honest, hard-working, reliable and loving man to share my life with – perhaps that is you. I am growing to love you too. Our ages are similar, you are 40 and I am 38. You are black and I am white, but that does not matter so long as we love, respect, and support each other. Also, we are both part of the wonderful Gratton Grange family which is an added benefit for a future together."

"You will move in?"

"Yes, I will tell Salina tomorrow."

Salina told her that she was pleased that the relationship continued to develop and wished them well. She also said that Joey's timber house could do with a face-lift, including new drapes and painting inside and out. Arrangements would be made for that to happen.

Soon after she moved in, Jessica asked Joey where his parents lived and when he last saw them.

"They live in a small house that they own in the New Orleans suburb of Metairie. I left school when I was 16 to become a field hand against my parents' wishes. I am an only child as my mother nearly died giving birth and was advised not to have any further children. They wanted the best for me, and that I should continue my education. There was quite an argument, after which I left home and moved into a unit in Cranton with a couple of buddies. I lost contact with my parents. But when I started working for Sam, he talked me into contacting them again. I last visited them about three months ago."

"What are their names and do they both work?"

"Roslyn and Grover. My mother works in a local supermarket and my father is employed by the local municipality in a team to maintain its parks and gardens."

"I would love to meet them. Why don't we visit them one afternoon soon? Can you arrange that?"

"I guess I could phone my mother, tell her about us and ask if we could visit."

"Joey, that would be great. I think it is important for our relationship. On another weekend we could visit my parents in Baton Rouge."

Both quite nervous, they arrived in Metairie mid-afternoon on a Sunday and parked in front of a small well-maintained terrace house with a pretty garden. Grover and Roslyn appeared in the doorway and greeted them with broad smiles and welcoming handshakes.

A long passage ran down one side of the interior, past a comfortable living room, the main bedroom, a second bedroom, a bathroom, and culminating in a surprisingly spacious kitchen that included a dining setting to accommodate six people. From the kitchen, a door led to a paved backyard with a couple of potted palms, a carport with a freshly polished Hyundai, a laundry, and an outdoor setting under a large umbrella.

Seated in the living room, Jessica chatted to Grover before Roslyn appeared with coffee and a platter of freshly baked cookies. Grover and Jessica did most of the talking including about his job tending to municipal gardens and her role at the restaurant. He was keenly interested in learning about the gardens that Salina had created and the general operation of Gratton Grange.

Jessica noted the tidiness and homeliness of the house with its comfortable furniture and photos on display including one of Joey in his school uniform. It was obvious that they were proud of their home. She also noticed the pretty floral dress that Roslyn was wearing, and her friendliness combined with a shyness that was quite attractive. It helped to project her pleasant personality.

As they drove home, Jessica told Joey that she thought his parents were lovely and that he should provide them with a little more of his time.

"I'm sorry that I was rather quiet, but I was apprehensive and worried about how the meeting would turn out. You have opened my eyes to my past inadequacy regarding my relationship with my parents, that they really do love me, and that I have a lot to make up for my neglect of them."

"That's OK Joey. I understand. We all make mistakes in life, but the main thing is that we learn from them. This visit has brought us even closer together," she said as she took his hand.

A few weeks later, as they were about to drive to Baton Rouge to visit Jessica's parents, Joey said he needed to talk to her first.

"As well as meeting your parents, I would like to introduce you to someone while we are in Baton Rouge."

"Oh yes, who is that?"

"My daughter."

"You have a daughter? When and how did that happen?"

"When I was seventeen, I met a girl of the same age at a party in Baton Rouge. We only went out a few times before Maria fell pregnant. It was quite a shock. She wanted to keep the baby, so I offered to marry her, but she declined and suggested we talk to her parents. They were Italian immigrants that I hardly knew."

"What happened then? Did they threaten to shoot you?"

"I was literally trembling with apprehension when I met them, but they were surprisingly calm and rational in the circumstances, which helped to put me more at ease. I think they appreciated that at least I turned up at the meeting. Her father Stephano looked at me intently. Not fiercely or threateningly, but seriously and firmly. He said Maria would continue to live with them. They were prepared to support and assist her when the baby arrived so that she could continue to work in the family's Italian restaurant in Baton Rouge. He also expected me to regularly contribute financially to the baby's upkeep."

"Did you continue to see Maria?"

"I spoke to her occasionally on the phone, and then she rang to invite me to an afternoon tea to celebrate Celeste's first birthday. After that I did not have contact again except for an occasional phone call. I just thought that it was better not to intrude into the settled situation, but I continued to provide regular financial support. I felt ashamed and significant guilt at the trouble I had caused for Maria and her family. Then one day Maria phoned and said she had told Celeste, who was now sixteen, that I was her father and that she wanted to meet me."

"Gee, what an amazing story. How did the meeting go?"

"Somehow I plucked up the courage and when I walked in the door of Maria's parent's home there was this attractive young lady who smiled and extended her hand. If I may say so, there was a definite likeness – she had my slender athletic build and a beauty born of her mother's Italian background and my black heritage.

"She simply said that for a long time she had been hoping to meet me one day, and I told her how happy I was that we had finally met. Maria and her parents said they had some shopping to do and would be back in about half an hour.

"I was keen to know about Celeste's life in Baton Rouge and what her plans were for the future. She told me that she was getting good grades at high school, that she was a member of the school basketball team and had recently been signed to play for the Baton Rouge Rockettes in the Louisiana State League. In relation to a future career, she said she would like to study pharmacy at university in New Orleans, to which I indicated that I would assist in whatever way I could, including financially."

"Did anyone know about this at Gratton Grange?"

"Soon after my meeting with Celeste I told Sam in confidence. He was very understanding and said that my secret must have been a heavy burden to carry for all those years. He added that he was proud of me for having done the honorable thing by confronting my responsibilities rather than avoiding the situation or running away. Do you still love me?"

"Yes, I do. I am also proud of the way you dealt with the situation. It would not have been easy. Do your parents know about Celeste?"

"I told them around the same time that I told Sam. They were shocked of course but pleased to suddenly learn that they had a granddaughter, who they have now met several times. Celeste is now 23 and following graduation now practices pharmacy at a major drugstore in Baton Rouge. She lives in a new condominium which she recently bought, and after several successful seasons with the Rockettes, is currently coaching a local junior team."

"I can't wait to meet her, and we had better get moving - perhaps we should visit Celeste first and then go on to meet my parents."

Jessica was taken aback by the tall stunning young woman dressed in tight-fitting active wear who opened the door of the two-story condominium. She literally bounced out to greet them with a huge smile, hugged Joey and then Jessica and ushered them inside for coffee. Jessica told her about meeting her grandparents recently in Metairie and how welcoming and nice they were.

"Oh yes, they are such wonderful genuine people. I am so lucky and pleased that I finally met them, and now I have also met you. My family continues to grow. It is exciting."

Celeste was a picture of vitality and happiness. Her words flowed effortlessly, given added emphasis by constant hand gestures. After about an hour Joey said they had to go meet Jessica's parents, to which Celeste responded with a big smile: "That is excellent, more additions to our family." As they left, Jessica hugged Celeste warmly and said she would be in touch soon to invite her for dinner at Gratton Grange.

Wayne and Nanette operated a small real estate business in Baton Rouge. Jessica had already told them about moving in with Joey and they were pleased to meet him at last and chat about his role as assistant manager at Gratton Grange. Then she told her parents about the delightful meeting they had just had with Celeste.

With a surprised laugh, Nanette said they knew Celeste's grandparents and her mother Maria through dining at their restaurant.

"Everyone in Baton Rouge knows of Celeste. She is quite a celebrity, especially because of her outstanding achievements on the basketball court," she added.

Wayne commented on Celeste's lovely outgoing personality and how well regarded she was in her work as a pharmacist.

"Joey, the way you have dealt with the challenges of your journey is a credit to you. I am glad our daughter is happy and is with an honorable man."

On the way back to Gratton Grange, Joey and Jessica agreed that they should meet with Sam and then tell Jack and Salina about Celeste.

A few months later, Grover retired at sixty from the Metairie Council. Sam offered him a part-time three days per week job tending the gardens at Gratton

Grange. Arrangements were made for him and Roslyn to move into the unit at the restaurant that had been vacated by Jessica. They leased-out their house in Metairie as Roslyn could not bear to sell it. She was pleased when Jessica invited her to do some waitressing and sometimes help in the kitchen at the restaurant.

CHAPTER 22

Now seventeen and recently graduated from high school in New York, Marcus phoned his father and told him that he wanted to live in New Orleans.

"I am keen to commence a degree course in agricultural science and have applied for a place at Southport University in New Orleans. It is a relatively new university with a strong emphasis on agriculture and commerce. I also understand that it has a very ethnically diverse student mix, which appeals to me. Do you like my plan?"

"You should go for it. There are lots of good opportunities relating to agriculture in Louisiana, so you have chosen a good career path. What area of agriculture do you plan to focus on?"

"At high school I received good grades in biology and science. After talking to those teachers, I did a lot of reading about developments in plant pathology and entomology. Those are the areas that I would like to pursue."

"That sounds like a good way to go. Those areas are certainly relevant to our operations at Gratton Grange. Where do you plan to live? You are of course welcome to stay at Gratton Grange, but I suspect you may wish to be more independent and located closer to the center of city action."

"I would like to take up student accommodation in an apartment near or on the university campus. I think that would be good, initially at least. Would it be OK if I fly down and stay with you and Salina until my place at the university is confirmed?"

"Sure, we would love that. You could earn a few dollars helping around Gratton Grange until you start your studies. I will talk to Sam about that."

Marcus was excited and rushed to tell his mother who helped him pack a large case and then drove him to the airport. As he waited to board, she hugged him tightly, told him how much she loved him and to be sure to phone her when he arrived. Tears were flowing as she waved him goodbye.

Driving home, Laura consoled herself with the belief that all her efforts in guiding Marcus's schooling and general development had resulted in a young man she could be proud of. She was also pleased and grateful that her relationship with her partner continued to be strong and would help to fill the gap in her life left by Marcus moving to New Orleans.

On arrival in New Orleans, Jack and Salina were waiting to drive him to Gratton Grange where Beth had prepared his favorite Cajun seafood dish for dinner. The next day he met with Joey who he would work along-side in various areas of the plantation including weed control, fertilizer application, and construction of new trellising in the vineyard.

After an anxious three weeks, Marcus received a letter from the university advising that he had been accepted into agricultural science. Overjoyed, he rang his mother immediately to tell her the good news. Jack suggested that he should make enquiries about student accommodation without delay as demand could be high.

The following day Salina drove him to the university to arrange his enrollment and to enquire about accommodation. They inspected a furnished modern bedsit with a small kitchenette on the third floor of a university building that was purpose-built for student accommodation.

"This is a great location right on the edge of the campus. What do you think Marcus?"

"I think it is perfect. It has everything that I need. There is a bus stop nearby and I like the way the building is surrounded by attractive landscaped gardens. Look, over there is a barbeque area. I could invite you and father for lunch. We could do some steaks and have a competition about who is the best cook."

At the university administration office Marcus signed a lease for 12 months to begin in two weeks. Stopping at a bank in New Orleans on the way home, Salina introduced Marcus to the manager. An account was opened for him.

CHAPTER 23

They met in the main student cafeteria on Marcus's second day on campus. He was an athletic looking guy with a thick crop of dark hair and biceps bulging from under a tight T shirt.

Very cheerful, chatty and a bit pushy, he seemed to be popular and know just about everyone in the room. Plonking down next to Marcus at the long, crowded table, he introduced himself as Brendon Lefont.

"You look like a freshman. Where you from buddy?"

"Marcus Lansell from New York. I'm enrolled in first year agricultural science."

"A bit of a city slicker?"

"You might say that, but I wouldn't. City slickers, as you call them, would not be likely to enroll in agricultural science, would they?"

"I suppose not."

"What are you studying?"

"Second year commerce, which I must admit I just scraped into. I'm more into sport and having a good time than study, according to my father. I guess it's his right to comment, seeing as he is paying the bills. He has threatened lately to withdraw support. I've been told to pull my head in or else."

"Are you going to?"

"Thinking about it. Are you into sport?"

"Played some tennis at high school, but that's about all. What about you?"

"Apart from girls and partying, sport is the main thing that attracts me. I'm especially into athletics, football, sailing and trap shooting."

Marcus was having difficulty working out whether he liked Brendon or not. He was certainly an interesting, vibrant, and confident guy. But he also seemed to be very egotistical and self-centered. He decided to delve further.

"Why did you choose commerce?"

"My parents own the Great Southern Resort here, plus a boat hire business. They are trying to groom me to take over one day."

"If I may say so, it sounds like a rather challenging proposition for them."

"Well, yes. But I guess I'll have to knuckle down and earn my keep some time soon. Until then I reckon life is for living and doing enough to avoid flunking out at the end of this year. Does your family support you financially at university?"

"Yes, to some extent, but I also contribute by working at weekends and holidays at my family's plantation."

"Plantation? Where is that?"

Marcus suddenly had some doubt about whether to continue the conversation, but he decided to plough on anyway.

"Gratton Grange on the Mississippi near Cranton."

"Good heavens. My friends and I had lunch at Gratton Grange Estate restaurant last weekend. You are part of that family? Jack Lansell is a leading surgeon in New Orleans."

"He is my father. I must be going. My first lecture starts in 10 minutes."

"OK. Come back for a coffee and tell me how it went. I'll still be here."

Seated towards the back of the tiered lecture theatre, Marcus waited for the professor of agricultural science to appear at the lectern. His mind swept back to New York and how much he loved his mother and appreciated the secure upbringing that she had provided for him. He thought what a whirlwind the last few weeks had been. Sitting now in this university lecture theatre so far away from where he grew up – it was almost unbelievable.

After the lecture, which lasted about an hour, he rejoined Brendon in the cafeteria.

"Well, were you impressed with your introduction to agricultural science, or was it just boring?"

"It was not at all boring. I found the scope of the course that was outlined for this year most interesting. It will cover areas such as land use, plant diseases common to Louisiana, insects and their control, and responsible use of weed killers. Have your commerce lectures started yet?"

"The first one is tomorrow which I may attend."

"That's not a very positive attitude to start the year with."

"Just kidding. I guess it's time to at least take some notice of my father's threat, just in case he really means it and I find myself out on the street."

"Do you live with your parents?"

"I have a bungalow behind their house, so I need to be careful that they don't change the locks. Are you doing anything next Sunday? A couple of friends and I plan to go for a leisurely sail Sunday afternoon. Would you like to join us?"

"I have to tell you that I have never been sailing, but I would certainly like to try it."

"Great. Can you swim?"

"I learnt when quite young in the pool at my grandparents' home on Long Island, New York. I am quite a capable swimmer."

"That's a good ability to have for your introduction to sailing, especially if you go over the side," Brendon said with a hearty laugh. "I have a car and will collect you at your lodgings around midday on Sunday. You will need boat shoes, a spray jacket, cap, sunglasses, and some sunscreen. Don't worry about lunch, I will look after that, or at least my mother will."

Waiting on the steps to the main entrance to his hall of residence, Marcus watched as a bright red drop-top Mustang screeched to a stop and Brendon leapt out.

"Hey there. All set to go?"

"I think so."

As he slid into the passenger seat Marcus commented on the heavy guitar riffs coming at high volume from the speakers.

"That's Howlin Wolf, one of my favorite blues musicians. I heard he will be playing at the House of Blues in New Orleans next month. You like blues?"

"Yes, blues and jazz. My father plays piano and his wife Salina, who I love almost as much as my mother, is a jazz and blues singer."

"Ah yes. Salina is great. She used to sing at Sirico's."

At that, Brendon planted his foot. From the rumble of the motor and the bark of the exhaust, it was obviously a V8. A puff of smoke came from the spinning tires as Marcus was thrown back sharply in his seat.

"Do you have any fears about being picked up by the police in this red rocket?"

"Sometimes. Last week I got another warning from the same officer, but he was almost friendly, saying I needed to be careful about pushing my luck too far."

"So, you are now being a bit more careful?"

"Sort of. I'm trying, but life is for living, isn't it?"

"Yes, within reasonable limits."

On the way Brendon explained that Lake Pontchartrain covers an area of some 630 square miles and forms the northern boundary of New Orleans.

"The boat that we will be sailing on today is an offshore sloop owned by my father. He uses it occasionally and sometimes hires it out. My friends and I use it more than my father - we often race it in handicap events."

Suddenly the water and clubhouse came into view. Brendon pulled into a shaded area of the carpark, and they walked into the reception area where Marcus signed in. On the upstairs verandah he was introduced to Harry and Matt who were also students at the university.

"Let's go boys," said Brendon. "I have a hamper, courtesy of my mother, and of course a cooler, that we need to collect from the trunk of my car."

They boarded the boat at a pen in the marina and placed the hamper and cooler in the cabin while Brendon fired up the motor. Marcus's first job was to catch the mooring rope as Matt threw it to him from the board walk, hold the yacht steady, and retrieve the fenders after Matt jumped aboard.

"Well done buddy," yelled Brendon, amid cheering and clapping. "I reckon there's a good chance we can make a sailor of you."

Once outside the marina they unfurled the jib. There was a good southerly breeze, so it was not long before Marcus helped Harry hoist the mainsail. He learnt the importance of observing changes in wind direction and making accurate decisions on when to tack.

They sailed around for about an hour including to Breakwater Park from where there were panoramic views across to the causeway which Brendon said was the longest continuous bridge in the world. Then they headed to the sandy Pontchartrain Beach where lots of people were enjoying the sun and picnicking.

"Let's drop anchor here. It's a great place for bird watching," said Brendon retrieving a pair of binoculars from the cabin.

"There seems to be a lot of birdlife. I noticed some pelicans and eagles at the park before," commented Marcus.

"Yes, but that's not the type of birdlife that I am thinking of," smirked Brendon, training the binoculars on the beach. "Have a look through these, especially to the left under the large yellow beach umbrella."

"Oh yes. I see what you mean, she is something to behold."

"The sun is now well over the yardarm, so I suggest it's time for some refreshments to celebrate the magnificent scenery around here," chuckled Brendon as he pulled a beer from the cooler.

"I hope nobody has got their binoculars trained on you right now. The police would certainly not be impressed," commented Matt.

"Having to wait until one is 22 before consuming alcohol without a parent present is a stupid law and should be repealed. If I am old enough at 18 to drive a car and vote, then I am old enough to drink a beer. What are they going to do, throw me in the slammer?"

"They might, depending on your general demeanor, which I suspect could be less than helpful in such a situation," said Matt, who was studying second year law at the university. "It could be the last straw for your father. You might even be disinherited," he suggested with a sly grin.

Brendon looked at Matt disapprovingly, gulped the beer down and offered one to Marcus who declined, saying he was not even 18 yet. Matt also declined, but Harry took the top off one and drank it in the cabin to avoid the possibility of prying eyes.

After further surveying the talent on the beach, Brendon opened the hamper basket provided by his mother to reveal an appealing array of items for lunch including chicken and avocado sandwiches, a cheese plater with biscuits, strawberries, grapes, and four bottles of Colorado Springwater.

Following lunch, they went for another sail. The wind was stronger, and Marcus had the challenging experience of helping to hoist the spinnaker. The yacht immediately picked up speed. At one point it was healing over so far that he took a tight grip on a handle mounted on the cabin roof. He was worried that they might capsize.

On the way back to the marina Brendon offered him a turn on the tiller to steer the boat, which he eagerly accepted.

"The tiller always moves in the opposite direction to which the bow of the boat is required to move. It will be confusing to start with and will take a while to get used to."

Suddenly, Matt yelled: "Watch out for that craft on our starboard side," and quickly pushed the tiller to change direction and avoid a possible collision.

A slightly shaken Marcus absorbed the lesson and continued with a keener eye and a firmer grip on the tiller. He was also given instructions about how to read the tell-tails on the sails that provide an indication of wind direction and wind changes.

As they approached the marina Brendon took over the tiller. Marcus noticed that he and Harry were sucking on mints to try to disguise any trace of alcohol on their breath.

Matt and Harry decided to stay on for a while at the clubhouse to catch up with some friends. Brendon said he was due home for a barbeque with his parents Gerard and Nora, and his sister Monica, who had recently turned sixteen. He invited Marcus to join them.

CHAPTER 24

They drove past the Great Southern Resort in the Garden District, which Brendon explained was run by a manager employed by his parents, before entering the winding driveway to his parent's home. It was lined with crepe myrtle trees in full bloom, and huge old oaks draped with moss that formed a canopy. A magnificent white mansion with a strong French influence came into view.

Gerard was a tall solidly built man in his late forties who smiled easily and greeted Marcus with a firm grip. They walked down a pathway to a sunken paved area with a rotunda surrounded by extensive manicured gardens where an elegant looking woman and a young girl sat.

"Hello, you must be Marcus. I'm Nora and this is Brendon's sister Monica."

Monica was an attractive young girl with dark hair like Brendon. Marcus noted that was where the similarity seemed to end. She appeared reserved and somewhat shy, while Brendon was often brash and egotistical. He could sense her inspecting him under her long lashes, with a slightly bowered head.

"How did your introduction to sailing go?" enquired Nora.

"It was most enjoyable, but I found that I was faced with a steep learning curve. The experience was very relaxing and at other times quite challenging. It is a challenge that I would very much like to pursue. Also, thank you so much for the lovely lunch that you prepared for us mam."

"It was a pleasure. Please call me Nora, and my husband is Gerard."

"Marcus, you are welcome to continue to sail regularly on that boat," Gerard said. "It is quite quick and not exactly built for learners. However, Brendon and his friends that you sailed with today are competent sailors, so you will learn a lot from them. Later, you might even join them in a club handicap race."

"Thank you, I would love to do that."

"I understand your father is Dr Jack Lansell. I know him well as we are both members of a Rotary Club in New Orleans. He is an outstanding person; a valued contributor to the local economy, our society generally, and especially the needs of the less fortunate."

"Thank you for your kind comments. This is a beautiful property. Does your family history go back a long way in the development of New Orleans?"

"My grandfather immigrated here from France and bought a plantation that mainly grew vegetables and some fruit for the greater New Orleans community. This very site was once part of that plantation. As the economy and population of New Orleans grew the plantation was subdivided by my father. He kept this property, which included the house where we now live, and the piece of land which is now occupied by the Great Southern Resort that my family owns."

"That's a fascinating family history. I love the abundance of French architecture in New Orleans, of which your home is an excellent example."

"We are proud of our home. After dinner we will show you around. I had better fire up the barbeque so we can start cooking. You are from New York, so we have some prime New York cut steaks to throw on the hotplate."

When Nora and Monica went into the house to finish preparing some salads, Gerard took the opportunity to ask Marcus about his university studies and plans for a future career.

"I have always had an interest in anything related to agriculture, starting with my own small garden at my grandparent's home on Long Island. Now, I really appreciate being able to participate in some of the activities at Gratton Grange. After graduation, I would like to pursue a career in agricultural research."

During the earlier conversation Marcus had noticed that Brendon had remained quiet, pretending to be disinterested. Now his demeaner suddenly changed. Perhaps he was starting to anticipate the direction that the conversation might take, and what could follow.

"You seem to have worked out the general direction that you would like your future to take. I believe it's about time that Brendon did the same instead of leaving all the worrying to Nora and I."

"That is not a fair thing to say…", started Brendon, but he was interrupted by Marcus.

"I have only known Brendon for a short time since my arrival in New Orleans, but I already regard him as a good friend. He did tell me that he believed it was important not to take life too seriously, to enjoy ones-self, and that worrying about the future could wait. However, out sailing we talked a little about the various operations at Gratton Grange and I said he should come and visit for a weekend."

"Brendon, that is an excellent offer from Marcus. It would be a great opportunity to experience what life is like on a working plantation. Are you going to take up the invitation?"

"I can feel some pressure coming on here, but yes, I would like to go. Thank you again Marcus for the invitation. When do you have in mind?"

"What about next weekend? I will talk to my father and Salina, as well as Sam, the manager of the plantation, about you and I helping out in various areas and earning some dollars."

Brendon looked quickly at Marcus and his father at the mention of 'helping out', gulped, and said rather unconvincingly that he looked forward to the experience.

Just then Nora and Monica arrived with the salads.

"What have you guys been cooking up, apart from those great looking steaks," asked Nora.

Brendon thought the best strategy was to jump in first with a response.

"I have been invited to spend next weekend helping out at Gratton Grange. I suspect this may be a conspiracy aimed at modifying my supposed playboy tendencies by getting my hands dirty for a change. But that's OK – I'm already starting to adjust and maybe some manual labor won't do me any harm."

Monica, who had hardly uttered a word until then, chipped in with: "The term 'playboy' about you is not 'supposed', it is a fact."

"That will be enough thankyou Monica," responded Nora.

After finishing their meals at a table in the rotunda, Nora suggested that they move to the house for a pavlova desert followed by coffee.

Inside the mansion the French influence was everywhere including in an abundance of beautiful period furniture. Huge hand-crafted tapestries and numerous oil paintings in heavy gold gilt frames adorned the walls. In the main sitting room was a grand piano that Nora said Monica was learning to play. Ceiling fans whirled throughout the house.

As Brendon drove him in the Mustang back to his hall of residence at the university, Marcus asked if he was OK with all the discussion about his attitude and future.

"Look buddy, I'm aware that I have to pull my head in to some extent. I guess I now need to lead a more balanced life. I understand that I am in a privileged position and that to some extent maturity and responsibility is being forced on me. But I do not want it to happen suddenly and lose my youth overnight. That is why I appreciate you as a friend, helping to ease my way forward."

"Brendon, you are a good friend and I really like your family. I reckon our somewhat different personalities will assist us to help each other as our lives move along. By the way, it was interesting how the discussion about you helped to bring Monica out of her shell," Marcus added with a laugh.

CHAPTER 25

Jack and Salina said they were happy to have Brendon as a guest for the following weekend. Sam indicated that there were numerous areas where the boys could work to assist Joey on the plantation for a couple of days.

Back at the university cafeteria Marcus conveyed the news to Brendon in the presence of Matt and Harry. He told him they would be required to meet with Joey at 8.00 AM next Saturday for a briefing on the work program for the weekend.

"You will need some old jeans and shirt plus a pair of work boots - Joey will provide gloves."

"I don't have any work boots."

"Well, you will have to buy some."

Harry suddenly burst out laughing. "Marcus, you will have to take some photos of the momentous occasion when Brendon is introduced to manual labor."

"You guys can laugh, but I see this as a great opportunity to experience a different aspect of life. I will think of you next weekend lounging around aimlessly while I do my bit to keep the economy of Louisiana ticking over."

"Jeez Marcus, how did you manage to achieve this amazing transformation in our friend's attitude? It will be interesting to see if he is singing the same tune next week, and whether he will need a few days to recover," chortled Harry.

It was around 7.30 AM when they arrived at the manor house in the Mustang and were met by Salina.

"Hello boys. What a great looking car. Welcome to Gratton Grange, Brendon. Let me show you to your room before you and Marcus talk to Joey."

Marcus was already familiar with the range of activities at Gratton Grange, but Joey explained each of the operations to Brendon and how they contributed to the overall success of the business.

Then Sam appeared unexpectedly. He emphasized how important it was for all elements of the business to contribute to making a profit for the company.

"We cannot tolerate loss-makers, at least not for long. Making a profit enables us to plough more back into the business, which in turn means the opportunity to make further profits and to employ more people. For everybody's benefit, businesses need to make a profit, including us. Not just for Gratton Grange, but to assist the entire economy of our state of Louisiana. Some people denigrate the term 'profit'. They regard it as a dirty word, but without profits businesses such as ours would not be able to employ people and pay taxes. The government would not be able to provide community benefits such as hospitals and schools, as well as a range of social services to assist the not so fortunate. It is not always easy to make a profit. It often takes a lot of application, determination and risks, and quite a lot of hard work."

Brendon said he had heard similar views about the importance of private enterprise and profits in lectures at university. He appreciated the opportunity for some hands-on experience in the operations of a highly diversified plantation-based business.

Joey then took over and asked Brendon which areas he was most interested in. He nominated the vineyard, the citrus plantation and, interestingly, the restaurant. However, he was not so keen to get involved in the apiary operations.

"OK, we will do some pruning of the citrus trees and remove a few that are old and unproductive. We can then move on to the vineyard and do some pruning there. In the morning we can do some fertilizing of the vegetable crops. Marcus and I can continue with that, and I will arrange for Brendon to help in the kitchen of the restaurant from about 11.00 AM. The three of us can have a late lunch at the restaurant after the main crowd has left at round 2.30 PM."

Joey insisted they wore hats, and sunscreen was applied before they climbed aboard his pickup truck and headed to rows of mature citrus trees not far from the manor house. He explained why pruning was necessary to maintain the health of the trees and demonstrated how to effectively go about it.

After removing several old trees with the help of a backhoe, around midday they moved over to the vineyard. Salina was already doing some pruning and had brought sandwiches and mineral water for lunch.

Over lunch she explained to Brendon the various types of vines that were planted, their different characteristics, and why those varieties were chosen. She also outlined the requirements for running a successful vineyard – from planting through to harvesting, wine making, and marketing. Brendon was then taught the specific technique for pruning the vines.

At around 5.00 PM Joey announced that it was time to head back to the manor house to freshen up before dinner. On the way they called in to introduce Brendon to Jessica who said the restaurant was booked out for dinner as well as for lunch the following day.

"Brendon, your face is familiar, I believe you were here with some friends for lunch recently. We could certainly use another hand in the kitchen in preparation for lunch tomorrow if that is OK with you."

"Thank you. As you say, I recently had the pleasure of dining at this renowned restaurant. I look forward to the experience of helping in a busy restaurant kitchen."

Just before dinner at the manor house Jack was introduced to Brendon and asked him about his first day working on the plantation.

"Although I regard myself as quite a fit person, I have never felt so tired. The work was interesting, and I learnt a lot. I now have a real sense of achievement in doing something that clearly provides a worthwhile result for a day's hard labor."

"I am pleased to hear that, Brendon. Joey tells me that you applied yourself well to the tasks that were allocated to you. There will be plenty more opportunities for you to do some work at Gratton Grange if you would like to do that. You will be most welcome."

After dinner Jack and Salina retired to the lounge to watch some television and Joey headed home after telling the boys that he would see them at 8.00 AM. As they helped Beth to clear the table Marcus poured the small amount left in a bottle of Gratton Grange Merlot into a glass and handed it to Brendon.

"You will no doubt sleep well tonight, but this should also help. After working in the vineyard today we can't have you leaving tomorrow without at least tasting the produce."

Beth pretended not to notice as they finished clearing the table and stacking the dishwasher.

CHAPTER 26

At the university, training and selection trials were well under way for the upcoming intervarsity track and field championships. Brendon became a hot favorite for the 200 meters and 400 meters events. In addition, he had been selected to anchor the 4x400 relay team.

Brendon had run personal best times in the trials. Much was expected of him at the championships and his fan base was expanding rapidly, especially amongst female students. Some had even formed a cheer squad for him. There was a bounce in his step as he wandered around the campus. But when he met with Marcus, Matt, and Harry at a table in a corner of the cafeteria, he admitted to experiencing increasing nerves.

"With all the hype that is building up, what if I don't perform to expectations? It seems that almost everyone expects me to win every event that I compete in. I reckon I might have to leave town if I don't produce the goods."

"Don't be stupid," exclaimed Marcus. "I have been watching your very committed preparation. The times that you have been clocking are really good and you can expect them to get even better."

On the day of the championships in the New Orleans Sports Stadium, Brendon met with his three close friends and his coach Andre Bellinger for breakfast in the cafeteria. Andre was also a lecturer in the commerce department at the university and had a good understanding of Brendon's personality.

"I can't eat anything. I'll just have a long black coffee," murmured Brendon.

"You must eat something. Just try some toast with honey, it could give you an energy boost," Andre said as he walked to the counter to order.

Leaving Brendon at the table, they joined the queue for breakfast. Andre selected muesli for himself, and coffees, plus honey and toast for Brendon, while the others went for pancakes.

Brendon just looked at his breakfast for a while, took a hesitant bite, looked at the pancakes, then headed for the bathroom and threw-up. Andre went after him, put his head under a tap and reappeared a few minutes later with a rather pale-looking Brendon. He then left and returned with some medication to settle Brendon's stomach from the university pharmacy, which he assured those at the table was 'absolutely legal'.

As the start time for the 200 meters approached, Andre did his best to help Brendon relax and told him that the only person that could beat him was himself. The field moved forward to place and adjust their starting blocks. They all did some trial starts except Brendon, who just stood there looking down the track, not even able to acknowledge the crowd of supporters. Andre was concerned, but knew he had an outstanding finish once he got into a rhythmic stride.

In the third inside lane, he got off to a poor start but by the halfway mark had made up ground and went to the line to win by a small margin. His cheer squad pranced out into the center of the stadium, waiving their streamers, chanting **GO BRENNY GO;** almost upstaging the university's official cheer squad.

The 400 meters was scheduled for mid-afternoon with a strong field of competitors representing universities from several southern states.

Andre had spent a lot of time coaching Brendon on how to run a 400 meters race which he regarded as one of the most challenging events in track and field. The different phases of the event were explained to him. Rapid acceleration out of the blocks over the first 50-70 meters was critical, then settling to a near maximum speed to conserve energy, before lifting with explosive pace with about 150 meters to go and finally, ensuring a strong forward thrust for the line.

This time Brendon was feeling more confident after his victory in the 200 meters and got off to a much better start. At the half-way mark he took the lead and was never headed as he powered to the line, setting a record for the event. The high-volume chant from his cheer squad was taken up by the large crowd of Southport students and reverberated around the ground.

The last event for the day was the 4x400 relay and the atmosphere was electric with excitement. The four-man team listened to some final advice and words of encouragement from Andre and then the starter's instructions. Before the start, Brendon told his team members: "We can do this, just don't drop the bloody baton."

As the third runner passed the baton to Brendon the team was running second last in a bunched field with a significant gap to the leader. Although it would mean he would have to run a longer distance, Brendon decided to go around the outside of the field and try to peg back the leader. He gave it everything he had, spurred on by the deafening cheers and screams from the crowd. The leader was weakening. Stride-by-stride he gathered him in, charged at the tape with his chest out, and with a mighty thrust threw himself across the line.

It was a photo finish. When the announcement came over the public address system that Southport had won, applause erupted for a brilliant and gallant effort. Brendon and his teammates were swamped with congratulations and soon after it was announced that the university had won the intervarsity track and field championship for the first time by a narrow margin. Andre was ecstatic at the achievement and extremely proud of the team. As an African American he was particularly pleased that two members of the relay team were also black. For him, it was another prominent example of successful integration within Southport's highly diverse student population. He was also impressed with the leadership abilities which were gradually being displayed by Brendon.

After his success in coaching athletics, Andre was appointed assistant coach of the university football team. In one game against Grandview University in Alabama, Brendon injured one of the opposition's top players in a fierce tackle and the player was carried from the field. At the end of the game Brendon had to be escorted back to the change rooms as the opposition's supporters, especially the girls from the Grandview cheer squad, were baying for his blood. Insults were hurled by supporters on both sides and for a while the situation looked like it could get out of control.

After the game Andre took him aside and spoke to him quietly.

"Brendon, you have enormous talent as an athlete and good potential academically if you can learn to focus and apply yourself better. You have become an absolute star at Southport and idolized by many. However, there is a need now to recognize that you also have a growing responsibility as a role model, not only within the university but also within the broader community. My family struggled to provide me with a good education which I appreciate and value immensely. You have the benefit of coming from a privileged background which is providing you with an easier path in life, but there is also an enormous opportunity to use that in a constructive way. I suspect you are only slowly starting to recognize that."

"Andre, I owe you so much. Over recent times I believe I have grown a lot, but still have some way to go. Maybe I need less arrogance and more consideration of others."

"You are a good guy, but that reckless block that you laid was absolutely unnecessary and not in the best interests of the sport. We deserved the penalty that resulted, and we deserved to lose the game."

CHAPTER 27

W hen Marcus turned 18 a party was held for him at the Gratton
Grange Estate restaurant which was closed to the public for the
private event.

Now he was legally able to drink alcohol, at least in the presence of his
parents. Brendon's parents were also invited, so that cleared Brendon to legally
have a glass or two. Marcus's mother Laura was there and stayed at the manor
house.

The Big Easy Band played, and the Mississippi Princess brought guests
from New Orleans and Baton Rouge, including Celeste. Some came from the
nearby town of Cranton, including the editor of the Cranton Chronicle, Barry
Blake.

Gerard took the opportunity to talk to Jack and thank him for providing
opportunities for Brendon to do some work at Gratton Grange.

"Jack, I believe that the real-life experience that he has gained here at Gratton Grange has had a significant influence in assisting to improve his attitude
to what he might want out of life and what he can contribute to society generally. His mother and I were becoming quite concerned about his limited sense
of responsibility. To some extent we blamed ourselves for perhaps spoiling
him and not being firmer in denying his requests, such as in the provision of
that Mustang. An important factor in the improvement in this whole scenario
is the friendship that has developed between Brendon and your son Marcus –
it has helped to expose him to a more grounded and expanded view of life."

"Brendon is a fine boy, Gerard. From what I have seen and heard, he is
only just starting to flourish and head towards reaching anything like his full
potential. I am really pleased that he and Marcus have become close buddies."

After his outstanding athletic performances, many girls were seeking Brendon's attention. There was one in his commerce lectures that he fancied, but
she was not impressed with his flamboyant manner. Louise ignored his

advances until one afternoon, leaving a lecture, he took the opportunity to ask her to join him for coffee in the cafeteria. Initially she said she needed to work on an assignment, but he talked her into joining him.

"You are from Baton Rouge?" he asked.

"I was born there. My father runs the family construction company, and my mother is a receptionist at a dental clinic."

"Do you have any brothers and sisters?"

"Just a younger sister, Isabella. I think my father always wished that I were a boy. But seeing as I am not, he is determined to make do with me as a possible heir apparent. That is why I am pursuing a commerce degree at Southport."

"That's interesting because my family has a similar view about my future. Unfortunately, I have not been living up to expectations. Some people think that I am more likely to be disinherited than become an heir apparent. They regard me as somewhat irresponsible, and just after a good time at my parents' expense."

"Do you think there might be some truth in that? You do have a reputation as a lover of the good life."

"I have been told to have a serious look at myself and to smarten-up. I am trying, and there is gradual improvement, I think. Are you happy being the heir apparent?"

"I'm quite enjoying my commerce studies and just doing my best to lay a foundation to hopefully be a success in life, whether that be in my family's business or in some other area."

"Look who just walked in the door. This guy is my best friend and is generally regarded as a steadying influence on me, especially by my family."

Brendon introduced Louise to Marcus, told her that he was studying agricultural science, and that his family owned Gratton Grange.

"Marcus, Louise and I were just discussing that she and I are expected by our families to eventually take over the family businesses. Have you ever felt like an heir apparent?"

"No. My focus at the moment is on completing my education at Southport and then hopefully landing a job in agricultural research."

Even though he had just met her, Marcus was impressed with Louise and felt that she could perhaps be a good influence on Brendon.

Over the next few months Brendon and Louise spent a lot of time together and became very fond of each other. He took her sailing, including for a picnic on an island in Lake Pontchartrain, and they often had dinner together, including at Sirico's. As time went by Marcus noticed his friend's personality softening - becoming less brash and egotistical.

It was late and raining one night as Brendon and Louise drove in the Mustang from a party for Harry's birthday at the apartment that he shared with Matt near the university. A large dog appeared in the middle of the road. In a reflex action Brendon swung the wheel and the Mustang slid sideways. The lamp post shook as the car struck and the sound of the impact reverberated around the nearby streets. Concerned residents rushed to the scene. The passenger side door and windscreen pillar had taken a heavy hit. An ambulance soon arrived with lights flashing and siren blaring. A shaken Brendon helped to extract Louise through the driver's doorway.

Conscious but unsteady on her feet, Louise was placed on a stretcher and action was taken to stem blood streaming from a cut above her eye and lacerations to her arm caused by broken glass. Marcus, who had also been at Harry's party, arrived on the scene as she was placed in the ambulance. He phoned his father and Brendon's parents to tell them what had happened. By now police were in attendance and questioning Brendon.

"Hello Brendon. You, again."

"Hi Constable Gregson, it wasn't my fault."

"It never is of course. Were you speeding?"

"No, I was well within the speed limit because of the wet conditions. I took evasive action to miss a dog that suddenly appeared from nowhere and this is the awful result.

"Have you been drinking?"

"No, I just want to go with Louise to the hospital."

"You will need to submit to a preliminary breath test. Please blow into this device until I tell you to stop."

The test showed a negative result and Brendon was able to join Louise in the back of the ambulance. On arrival she was given a full medical examination including X Rays of her head which revealed a fractured and depressed eye socket that would need surgery.

Jack had phoned the hospital to check on her condition and it was agreed that he would immediately come to perform reconstructive surgery.

Brendon struggled to hold back tears as he held her hand and looked at her bruised and swollen face.

"I am so sorry Louise."

"It was not your fault. At least we saved that dog's life. I hope I don't miss too many lectures."

"Don't worry, I will take plenty of notes and provide you with copies."

Brendon was then asked to leave while she was prepped for the operating theatre.

After the surgery Jack told Louise that he was pleased with the result.

"It was quite a delicate and challenging procedure. My main concern was to ensure that your eye was fully protected as I reconstructed the area around it, including damage to the socket structure and some nerves that were also impacted. I am sure you will soon be able to look in the mirror and there will be little if any evidence of what happened. However, you will need to take it easy for a while as there is some indication of concussion."

"Thank you so much Dr Lansell. I just want you and others to know that it was not Brendon's fault. That dog should not have been out on the road."

"I understand that the police also believe that the dog was the cause of the accident and that no action will be taken against Brendon."

Louise's parents, Rick and Lorie Mangan, were understandably extremely upset about what happened to their daughter. Rick was quite a tough business-man who had started in the construction industry in Baton Rouge as a builder's laborer, then went out on his own building affordable homes on the edge of the city. Now his family controlled a successful business constructing major projects in Louisiana, including multi-story accommodation.

As he left the room Jack saw Rick and Lorie seated in the corridor. He introduced himself and told them that the operation went well and that she should make a full recovery.

"Doctor, we are most grateful to you for looking after our daughter. As for the driver of the car, I am looking at commencing litigation against him," said an agitated Rick.

"Rick, Louise has told me that Brendon was not responsible for the accident. That has now been confirmed by the police. I have observed that Brendon is extremely upset about the situation, that he is very fond of your daughter, and that she is strongly supportive of him."

When they went into the room, Rick held her hand and then made some negative comments about Brendon which drew a strong defensive response from Louise and led to Lorie rebuking him. Brendon was sitting outside as they left and rose to introduce himself, but Rick ignored him and kept walking. Concerned at his lack of common decency, Lorie approached and extended her hand.

"I am pleased to meet you, Brendon. Do not worry about Rick, he is just a grumpy father who needs to calm down and look at things more rationally. When Louise is fully recovered you must visit – we will have a nice lunch."

CHAPTER 28

On discharge from the hospital, Louise went to her parent's home in Baton Rouge to recuperate. Her condition rapidly improved and Brendon phoned her each day to check on progress. Then, after consultation with Louise, Lorie announced to Rick that Brendon had been invited to lunch the following Sunday. At first, he had said he did not want him in the house, but after a barrage of responses from the two women, including that he was being extremely unreasonable and dogmatic, he grudgingly relented. His gradually mellowing disposition had been helped by a recent phone call, soon after Louise left hospital, from Brendon's father Gerard who conveyed how sorry he was about the accident.

The Mangan family home, in a pleasant leafy part of the city, stretched across a large block on one level. It was an elongated ranch style with a verandah running along the entire front draped with fragrant blue wisteria in flower. It overlooked an extensive lawn that ran down to a huge well-trimmed hedge that provided complete privacy from the roadway. It was an impressive comfortable home rather than grand or ostentatious. Perhaps it reflected Rick's down-to-earth, no-frills personality.

The garden was not of any specific style. It was quite natural in character and Brendon later learned that Rick's favorite pastime was to ride his mower dodging around the many trees and bushes. The landscape echoed his masculine stamp rather than the influence of a woman. The only flowerbed was a small one next to the garage.

Louise, who was now almost fully recovered and displaying virtually no physical reminders of her ordeal, happily helped her mother set the table for lunch, including a bunch of flowers she had picked. She was excited but also apprehensive about what would happen when Brendon met her father.

Rick continued to work in his office as a Chevrolet SUV entered the driveway and parked in front of the large garage at one end of the house. Louise rushed to greet him with a welcoming hug and took his hand as they walked into the main living room where he was also warmly welcomed by Lorie.

They chatted for a while before Louise asked her mother: "Where is Pa?"

"In his office as usual, ensuring that we make another dollar tomorrow," she said loud enough for him to hear.

Soon after, Rick sauntered into the room with a casual and rather disinterested demeanor. Observing this, Brendon decided to take the initiative, walked up to him, extended his hand and said: "Pleased to meet you sir. I am so sorry that the accident has caused your family so much trouble and concern."

Forced to shake his hand, Rick responded: "Well at least I see you are now driving a more sensible and safer vehicle."

"You are right. The Mustang was a write-off and this time I took my father's advice and went for an SUV. The insurance payout covered the cost of the purchase, but I am required to pay for on-road costs as my father has tightened the purse strings. Thankfully, the occasional work that I am now doing at Gratton Grange is assisting with my outgoings, as well as some work at my father's boat hire business."

As they moved into the dining room, Lorie told Brendon: "By the way I am Lorie, and this is Rick - not 'mister' or 'sir'. I cannot foresee that he will ever be knighted," she said with a cynical smile. Rick gave her a quick sideways glance but said nothing.

Over lunch, Rick probed about Brendon's family background: "Does it go back to the French settlement in New Orleans," he asked.

"My great-grandfather moved there from France and bought a plantation which was later sub-divided. A section of the plantation is where my family now live and nearby is a holiday resort which we own," explained Brendon. "Were you born in Baton Rouge?"

Rick, now starting to relax and loosen-up, said with some obvious pride that his mother and father moved from New Orleans for better work opportunities when he was only two years old. "My father was good with his hands, and they were determined to make a better life for themselves. He got a job as a carpenter with a home-building company. I eventually joined the company as a laborer, and by that time my father was a site supervisor. Later I went out on my own building houses before establishing the construction company that we now operate. With the help of a very obliging bank manager, I might add. Our projects are now providing a significant contribution to the prosperity of Louisiana, especially in relation to employment creation."

"That is a very impressive family history. It shows lots of initiative and no doubt the need to take some calculated risks. Part of my university commerce course is about the challenges of starting a new business."

After some general discussion about the expanding economy of Baton Rouge, especially in the manufacturing and construction sectors, Lorie and Louise cleared the table and went to the kitchen to prepare a fruit salad.

Rick was now warming to Brendon's carefully expressed interest in business opportunities.

"When you finish university, do you plan to work in your family's businesses?" he asked.

"It could be an option and I believe that my parents would be happy for me to do that."

"It is also useful to get some experience in other areas, such as you are doing at Gratton Grange – it can help you to form views about various options for the future. If you are interested, we could look at providing you with some experience in the construction industry, perhaps during a university vacation."

"Thanks Rick, that is a very generous offer that I would like to pursue further with you."

At that point, Lorie and Louise returned to the table with a large bowl of fresh fruit salad together with a choice of cream or gelato, or both. Brendon went for both.

"Well, have you guys solved the problems of the world while we were busy in the kitchen?" asked Lorie with a hint of sarcasm.

"We have been discussing Brendon's views about a future career and I think we have agreed that he should investigate his options. I have offered him some occasional work with our construction company to help broaden his horizons."

Louise could not believe her ears at the apparent change in attitude by her father.

"Does this mean that I am no longer the heir apparent? Good heavens, what a relief," she said with a laugh.

"Don't be silly Louise. I am simply trying to help this young guy after a traumatic experience for him as well as our family."

Lorie just sat there quietly smiling. She was not surprised at the change in Rick. She knew her husband well. He was a man of strong principle who could form opinions quickly, but just as quickly change his mind if there was strong reason to do so. She was proud of his sudden change of tack.

It was late afternoon as he left. The blazing sun had descended and was resting on the treetops, casting long shadows on the lawn up to the house. Standing with Lorie on the verandah, Rick handed Brendon his business card and shook his hand. Louise walked with him to the Chevrolet. They kissed and hugged for an extended time, obviously intending to send a message. Driving away, he felt uplifted with happiness and optimism about the future.

Relaxing on a chair on the verandah overlooking his beloved expansive lawn, while Lorie and Louise chatted inside about how well the afternoon went, Rick thought about his changing attitude to Brendon.

He felt he had been rather impetuous about judging him so quickly. Lately, he had also been wondering whether Louise had the inclination to jump in at the deep end to help manage a major construction enterprise and eventually take over from him. Also, she seemed very close to Brendon and perhaps was genuinely in love with him. He pondered about the possibility that she could walk away if he continued an antagonistic attitude towards her friend. There was even a possibility that both women, Lorie, and Louise, could turn against him and cause a huge disruption if he had continued with a negative attitude.

Although Brendon was quite young, over lunch Rick had seen a lot of confidence and a hint of astuteness – qualities that could be tapped and would be valuable in the construction industry. Also, if he was truthful with himself, he was beginning to like the guy. It would be in everyone's interest – Louise, Lorie, himself, and Brendon - if he worked out a way to gradually introduce Brendon to the business as well as Louise. He realized that if he did not take appropriate action everything that he had worked so hard to create could be jeopardized – it was not a risk he was prepared to contemplate.

'There will be no favorites, I will treat them both equally', he thought, beginning to work out a master plan for the future.

CHAPTER 29

Jack's reputation as a leading reconstructive surgeon continued to grow. At the start of summer in Louisiana he was invited to deliver a keynote address to an international conference on reconstructive surgery in Darwin, Australia. In 'The Land Down Under' it was winter. The location was appropriate as the 'Top End' of the Northern Territory was prone to cyclones, including Cyclone Tracy which had devastated Darwin back in December 1974. Half of the city's inhabitants were left without a home, and 71 people were killed. A huge number of buildings were destroyed, and a large part of the city had to be rebuilt.

Salina suggested to Jack that he take Marcus and Brendon with him and that she would stay home with Eloise, who had recently commenced at high school in New Orleans.

"Jack, I think that the trip would be particularly good for Brendon. He has had a difficult time lately. It would be a great opportunity for he and Marcus to experience an interesting and different part of the world."

"That's a good idea. I will phone Marcus now and then speak to Gerard about covering the cost for Brendon."

Marcus was with Brendon watching a basketball game when Jack phoned. He was excited about the offer and said Brendon was also very keen and delighted to be asked. Jack then phoned Gerard.

"Thanks for the call, Jack. What a great opportunity," he said. "It's the type of break that Brendon needs right now, and we will of course cover his costs. The trip will contribute to his development, which along with his relationship with Louise, we are really pleased about."

Louise was also supportive and told him: "It will be my turn to take some lecture notes for you."

On arrival in Darwin, they checked into a suite at a hotel on the Esplanade and relaxed on the balcony overlooking an attractive tropical garden framed by huge palm trees. Across the roadway, expansive lawns swept down to Lameroo Beach on Darwin Harbour. Jack ordered a six-pack of Great Northern beer which they consumed while discussing an itinerary for the next two weeks.

The following morning Jack delivered the keynote address to a packed audience of delegates from around the world at the two-day conference. He outlined the scope of his experience and some of the big challenges that he had faced during reconstructive surgery. Information about techniques that he had developed in effectively dealing with a sudden influx of emergency patients was also provided.

Marcus and Brendon spent the day roaming around the central business district of Darwin and the waterfront precinct. The next day they visited the Darwin Yacht Club. They were welcomed by the locals, including Alex and his mate Burnie who owned a 40' keel boat that they used for cruising as well as racing.

"You blokes done any sailing?" asked a friendly, middle-aged Alex, squinting at them from a wrinkled weather-beaten face. "We are short of crew for a handicap club race on Sunday."

Marcus took the initiative. "Brendon is an accomplished sailor and experienced in keel boat racing in New Orleans. I have crewed in a couple of club races with him but must admit that I am still very much a keen learner."

"That sounds OK to me Marcus. There is a good chance that you will learn more on Sunday as our club events are extremely competitive. Can you both be on deck at 9.00 AM?"

They eagerly agreed as Burnie arrived with a round of beers. Alex explained that the course for the race would take around four hours to complete, and they talked about the likely weather conditions. The boys were also told to ensure they brought appropriate shoes, clothing, and protection from the sun.

After he delivered his address on the first day of the two-day conference, Jack listened to a couple of other presentations and then joined an expert panel for a question-and-answer session. During the buffet lunch that followed he took the opportunity to move around and talk to a range of attendees. He was particularly pleased when a senior surgeon at the main hospital invited him to tour the hospital facilities before he left Darwin. That night he attended the gala dinner which provided a further opportunity for networking amongst the delegates.

The following night, after the conference concluded, Jack and the boys met for drinks and dinner in Mitchell Street which was well known as the center of action in Darwin. The warm balmy weather reminded them of home as they watched the passing parade of people.

"This is a really interesting city," commented Marcus. "I'm surprised by the multitude of cultures – it's like a mixing pot of people from around the world, and they generally seem very relaxed and friendly."

"I love this town because there is a rawness about it," added Brendon. "A frontier spirit still exists here which is quite attractive, and there is a great assortment of characters. Alex and his mate Burnie who we met at the yacht club are good examples – tough but friendly guys who look you straight in the eye and tell it like it is. Blokes like that are 'the salt of the earth', as one of their mates told me at the club."

"You guys are already starting to talk like locals," commented Jack, finishing his meal and a glass of Adelaide Hills Riesling. "At this rate I'm worried I could be going home on my own."

The next day, Saturday, Jack suggested they should visit the Military Museum at East Point as he had heard that it provided an amazing insight to the attack on Darwin by the Japanese in February 1942 during World War II.

"The Japanese attacked Darwin? Clearly, they failed," said an astounded Brendon.

Marcus, who had been reading about the history of Darwin, decided not to comment and left the response to Jack.

"Let's take a bus to East Point and have a look around the museum. I understand we can view some graphic original film footage of what happened."

As they sat in a small picture theatre at the museum the flickering black and white film and loud soundtrack created an atmosphere which felt like they were watching an historic event in real-time. It was almost like the bombs were exploding around them.

Narration during the film explained that on one day 188 Japanese aircraft were in the first attack and 54 in a second attack, killing 235 people. The Northern Territory was raided 64 times and Darwin's Memorial Wall lists 1672 people who lost their lives in operations across Northern Australia. In central Darwin, a major target of Japanese bombers was the post office because it was a communications center. Ten postal and telegraph employees were killed when the post office was hit.

As they left the theatre, Brendon commented: "It's hard to believe what we just saw; that such an unprovoked attack happened in this peace-loving country on the other side of the world from where we live."

Jack then explained how the attack led to the Battle of the Coral Sea which decided Australia's fate in May 1942.

"The celebrated United States military man, General Douglas MacArthur, arrived from conflict in the Philippines. He was appointed Supreme Commander of all Allied Forces in the South-West Pacific, including US and Australian naval forces engaged in the Coral Sea battle. The Japanese lost the battle after sustaining heavy losses including two large aircraft carriers and numerous other battleships. To this day Australia and the US remain strong allies which is reflected in the ANZUS Treaty between Australia, New Zealand, and the US. Currently there is a significant US military presence stationed here in the Northern Territory. With a land mass the same size as the USA, Australia has a lot of area to protect and obviously any threat is going to come from the north."

"I have noticed several G I's around town and was talking to a couple in the supermarket near our hotel yesterday. They said they loved being here and that the US presence was important for both countries," said Brendon.

The following day Marcus and Brendon had their first taste of sailing off the Top End in Australia. There was a strong southerly blowing, so the crew were kept busy on *Sunburst* with several exciting tacks that included a close shave in a dual with another large yacht. Alex, who skippered *Sunburst,* later told the boys that he was a little nervous at the time because the other yacht was owned and skippered by the club commodore, who was a ferocious competitor.

Later, back in the club house, they were pleased when declared second placegetter in the race which was won narrowly by the commodore's boat. Congratulating the commodore on the win, Alex jokingly referred to the near collision and said he felt it best to bow to seniority in the circumstances and give way during the tacking duel.

"Alex, you scoundrel, you know damn well that if you hadn't backed-off I would have appealed and you would have been disqualified," responded the commodore.

Turning to Marcus and Brendon, Alex said: "Remember what I was saying the other day? There is an extremely competitive spirit at this club, which is why we love the place. What are your plans for the rest of your stay in the Top End?"

"Over coming days, we plan to check out the museum at Parliament House, visit the casino and the nearby Mindil Market, back a winner at the Darwin Cup, and then visit Kakadu," said Marcus."

"That should give you a good introductory feel for Darwin and surrounds. There is a lot to experience in the Top End. Some of the scenery and aboriginal art in caves around the countryside should be experienced, as well as the interesting fauna which includes wild camels introduced by Afghans to form camel trains in the early days of settlement. There are also introduced buffalo, and Australia's emu's which are large flightless birds that roam the landscape. We also have some of the most dangerous snakes in the world, not to mention those pesky crocodiles. If you plan to come back again maybe you would be interested in joining us for the midyear weekend regatta. Meanwhile Brendon, perhaps Marcus could get in some more competitive sailing experience with you in New Orleans."

In unison, Marcus and Brendon said they would love to do that and thanked Alex for such a great opportunity.

"Next time you should stay at my place at Cullum Bay where there is plenty of room for a couple of American adventurers. Marcus, I have been reading about the medical conference which has just concluded in Darwin and saw that your father delivered the keynote address. Before you return to the US maybe Dr Lansell would like to join us here at the club for dinner?"

"Thanks Alex, I'm sure my father would be delighted to do that. Maybe we could schedule it for when we get back from Kakadu, the last night before we leave."

CHAPTER 30

Heading south-east down the Arnhem Highway after renting a Toyota Landcruiser and a small gas barbeque, the three adventurers reflected on their previous day's experience at the Darwin Cup.

"Well, I'm quite happy," said Marcus, waving around five hundred dollars in cash.

Jack, who was driving, said he was about even on the day, and Brendon said he was down just under one hundred dollars.

"Marcus, obviously it's your shout for dinner tonight," said Jack, who was immediately supported by Brendon.

"Is that a custom in 'The Land Down Under' or is it something that you guys just dreamt up?" complained Marcus, quickly putting his cash away.

"Marcus, it's what mates do in this part of the world," said Brendon, smiling at Jack. Hey, Marcus, look at that big sign. It says there are 10,000 crocodiles in the Kakadu National Park. You had better open that wallet or we will feed you to the crocs."

"OK you guys, lets agree that I will pay for lunch rather than dinner because I reckon you blokes will go for it at dinner if I'm paying and run up a huge bill. Deal or no deal?"

There was silence for a while as Marcus shifted uncomfortably in his seat before, feigning disappointment, they agreed to the proposal.

After driving for nearly three hours, they pulled into a roadhouse on the highway just before Kakadu for lunch. Burgers with the lot, bowls of chips, and bottles of Top End spring water were consumed as they watched the growing flow of traffic pass by including camper vans and motor homes.

Looking at his companions with a smile from under a new Akubra hat that he had bought in Darwin, Marcus wanted to avoid any thoughts that he might be mean with his winnings.

"Seeing as you were kind enough to agree to my offer to pay for lunch, I will also get us some gelato for the road." Jack and Brendon decided it was time to ease up and thanked him sincerely for the enjoyable lunch, including the gelato.

At Yellow Water they checked into a motel which also had a bistro and bar plus a well-stocked store. Near the motel a young aboriginal man sat on an upturned bucket playing a digeridoo. Next to him lay a well-worn Akubra inviting people to acknowledge and remunerate the unique form of music that he was expertly producing. Next to the Akubra was a stick in the ground supporting a hand-written sign offering digeridoo sales and lessons.

They stood listening for a while before Marcus placed a contribution in the hat and introduced himself. He learned that the young man's name was Jimmy and arranged for a lesson later in the afternoon.

Moving along they bought some red bush apples and came across an old aboriginal man offering boomerang throwing lessons. Brendon was enthralled with how Billy, with nonchalant ease, was repeatedly able to deliver the boomerang to land back at his feet. He just had to have a try. After several less than impressive attempts he managed to at least get the boomerang to return in his general direction.

The one he bought was beautifully carved and painted. Billy told him that over the many centuries of aboriginal existence in Australia, boomerangs were often used by hunters to bring down prey such as kangaroos.

"You will learn this, but you must keep practicing when you return to your deep south. I have shown you how to hold it and how to throw it. Practice, practice, practice."

"Thank you, Billy, and please give me another two boomerangs so that my mates and I can practice together when we get home. We will have a throwing competition."

By now Marcus had returned to see Jimmy for his didgeridoo lesson. As they returned to the motel for dinner, the haunting sounds of digeridoos greeted Jack and Brendon. There was Marcus seated on an upturned bucket next to Jimmy. He was concentrating so much on absorbing the lesson that he failed to notice that they had arrived.

As the lesson ended, the small crowd that had gathered clapped, and an embarrassed Marcus shook hands with Jimmy and did an exaggerated bow to the observers.

Marcus decided to buy a digeridoo and introduced Jack and Brendon to Jimmy who asked what they were doing for dinner.

"I can provide an excellent bush tucker dinner at a very reasonable price if you are interested."

Jack said they had already reserved a table for dinner at the bistro but, looking at the others, suggested they should have bush tucker with Jimmy the following night. Brendon and Marcus were a little hesitant, but it was finally agreed.

Next day they took a cruise on the Yellow Water billabong in a large flat-bottom boat with an overhead canopy. A young black boy was selling water lily hats on the jetty.

"G'day everyone. You will need these water lily hats for your cruise in today's hot sun. They are strong and waterproof. Very 'cool' and cooling."

A multi-national group of tourists boarded. Many were wearing the 'cool' hats.

The guide explained that the cruise provided a unique opportunity to observe the enormously varied birdlife of Kakadu's World Heritage wetlands. He advised everyone to remain seated, away from the sides. Croc's, he said, had been known to leap out of the water, propelled by the strength of their long powerful tail, latch onto an unfortunate person in a boat, and drag them into the water.

They cruised along through huge swathes of water lilies with glorious red and white flowers. The guide pointed out a wide variety of bird species including lorikeets, rosellas, finches, and robins, as well as a pair of brolgas dancing, much to the delight of the passengers. There were also many magpie geese, green pygmy geese, whistling ducks, Australian pelicans, herons, and long-legged storks searching amongst the water lilies for food.

"This is a wonderful place for birds because Kakadu has many different habitats such as monsoon forests, mangroves, savanna regions, and flood plains where buffalo also roam. Many migrating birds come here to rest, feed and breed," the guide explained.

"We are now approaching a small billabong within this enormous Yellow Water billabong. On the bank you will notice a huge old crocodile that has some injuries around the head area, probably as a result of a fight with another crocodile over territory. Near him, lying quietly in the water, is a much smaller crocodile. She is his girlfriend and is protecting him in his time of need."

The tourists were fascinated at viewing a real-life love story between two prehistoric creatures. Predatory birds hovered expectantly overhead while the eyes of some interested crocs nearby glistened, just above the water. The girlfriend slowly shifted this way and that, watchful, and ready to repel a sudden attack on her injured mate.

But life was still evident. He snapped his huge jaws, revealing some broken teeth, and swished his long tail as if to say: 'Advance at your peril'. One half-open eye kept watch on the water. A bird landed on his back, picking tiny insects and growths while flies congregated on his wounds.

"I reckon that's one smart old croc," commented Marcus. "He's resting against a rocky outcrop so that he can't be attacked from the rear."

Arriving back at the motel late afternoon they freshened up, bought a slab of Great Northern beer at the store, and then met Jimmy at his caravan. The Landcruiser was loaded with provisions that he and one of his mates had gathered for the bush tucker dinner, plus didgeridoos, and some clapsticks.

They drove for only about twenty minutes before coming to a clearing in tropical forest near a small billabong. Brushing away bush flies with a wave of his hand in traditional Aussie salute fashion, Jimmy prepared a fire pit where he would roast, on hot coals, some freshly caught barramundi wrapped in leaves. Before the main dish was put on the coals though, he handed around some bowls of witchetty grubs which he explained were found in plant roots and have an appealing nutty taste, as well as some sweet-tasting honey ants.

"I'm going to need something to settle my nerves before I try this tucker," declared Brendon, reaching for a bottle of Great Northern. Marcus and Jack agreed.

Jimmy said that while bush tucker could be a challenge when first tried, it had many benefits.

"You can eat these raw or threaded and roasted on some wires that I have brought. I prefer eating them raw after removing the head," he said swallowing a grub that was still wriggling.

"This fantastic food is high in nutritional value including protein and fiber, and low in sugar and glucose. Also, many native plants and foods are used in bush medicine. All the bush tucker you will have tonight is really good for you," he said, swallowing a couple of honey ants and licking his lips.

After several gulps of Great Northern, Jack decided to lead the way, threw his head back and chewed down on a sizable headless witchetty grub followed by another gulp of beer.

"Come on you blokes, what are you waiting for. It helps if you close your eyes and chew quickly," advised Jack.

Not wanting to be accused of lacking intestinal fortitude, the boys each tried a witchetty grub.

"I think I can feel it still wriggling in my stomach," said Brendon, looking slightly uncomfortable.

"Rubbish," said Marcus, now munching on a honey ant. "It's just your vivid imagination at work. Have another beer if you are so concerned – maybe you can drown it," he suggested sarcastically.

"Dr Lansell, I am pleased that you seem to be feeling OK, as we may need you to pump out our stomachs," said a half-serious Brendon.

"Brendon, the only reason you may need me to do that is because of all the beer you two blokes have been drinking. I think it's time for us to try the barramundi that Jimmy is cooking on the coals."

After a delicious meal of barramundi, followed by a mixed bowl of bush bananas, wild watermelon, cockle berries and nuts, Jimmy handed Jack and Brendon some clapsticks as the sun descended and an almost full moon appeared.

"These instruments are used by striking one stick on another to maintain rhythm, including during didgeridoo playing. You can accompany Marcus and I while we play the didgeridoos."

As they played in the glow of the firepit, a dingo howled some distance away, answered by another that seemed much closer. Jimmy suggested that the wild dogs were responding in appreciation of the ancient music that floated eerily in the night air, creating a strange spiritual atmosphere.

Before leaving to drive back to Darwin the next morning, they gave Jimmy a generous payment for the way he had looked after them and thanked him for an unforgettable experience.

As they left the Kakadu National Park, they decided to have lunch beside a river near the main highway. It was a quiet, pretty spot, surrounded by tropical vegetation. The only others around were an elderly couple nearby from Sydney who had slept there in a motor home.

They introduced themselves to Eric and Edith and were welcomed by Rusty, their frisky red kelpie dog which was on a leash tied to the motor home steps.

Jack removed the portable barbeque from the Landcruiser and began cooking three kangaroo steaks, that he had bought from Jimmy, while the boys set up camp chairs.

Suddenly, Rusty saw a small wallaby down at the water having a drink, became excited, slipped his collar, and rushed down to the water's edge. The wallaby took off in fright. A crocodile which had lined up the wallaby for lunch, suddenly launched out of the water at lightning speed and snapped its jaws around the frantically yelping dog. Eric grabbed a tent pole and dashed towards the water hoping to force the croc to release the dog. Rusty, shaken violently from side to side, was now limp in its mouth. Marcus and Brendon moved quickly to drag Eric back as the croc disappeared into deeper water with Rusty.

Edith was beside herself, screaming and crying. Jack sat her down and administered a sedative to calm her. He then walked over to Eric who was now sitting on the motor home steps with his head bowered and handed him a beer from a cooler in the Landcruiser.

With a weak voice and tears in his eyes, Eric said how he loved the dog which they had taken with them when they retired from their farm to a property on the northern beaches of Sydney.

"That dog was truly an integral part of our family. This is going to leave a huge hole in our lives."

"Eric, where did you obtain Rusty?"

"He came from a specialist kelpie breeder on a property near Newcastle, north of Sydney."

"Can I suggest that you drive to the breeder soon after you get home and purchase another Rusty. You may not believe it right now, but another dog will help soothe the pain for you and Enid."

"We are so glad that you are here providing a shoulder to lean on. With our farming background, we know how important dogs are. I once had another kelpie that, as it got older, developed mange, and eventually had to be put down. I could not do it, but our neighbor offered to undertake the task. He told me to tie Skipper to a tree and walk away. I kissed that wonderful dog and will never forget the sound of the gunshot as it echoed up the valley."

"Eric, we need to continue our journey back to Darwin. Can I suggest that you and Enid pack up here and follow us to a small town nearby with a caravan park that we noticed on our way down from Darwin. Alternatively, you are welcome to follow us to Darwin."

Looking at Enid, who was now quite drowsy from the medication, Eric decided to stay overnight at the local caravan park. After seeing them settled on a site and exchanging contact details, Jack and the boys headed to Darwin.

CHAPTER 31

On their last day in Darwin, they had lunch at a Waterfront Precinct café before packing for the long trip home the next day, and then walking to the yacht club for dinner.

Alex and Burnie were already there – Burnie with a stylish middle-aged brunette who he introduced as his wife Marjorie, and Alex with an attractive young blonde.

There were introductions all round, including Alex proudly presenting his daughter Naomi to the visitors from America.

"After I told Naomi about the guys from New Orleans who sailed with us recently, she has been pestering me to meet you, and also Jack, who she read about in the local media during the recent medical conference," said Alex putting his hand on Jack's shoulder.

Over a round of drinks Jack answered a lot of questions about life in New Orleans and at Gratton Grange. Burnie was keen to know whether they had enjoyed their stay in the Top End.

Brendon was quick to say what a great time they had, including the opportunity provided by Alex and Burnie to take part in a yacht race, learning about the attack on Darwin during the war, and experiencing the wonders of Kakadu. He then went on to describe what happened to Rusty on the return journey from Kakadu.

"Marcus and I are looking forward to coming back again next year for the regatta. We want to see more of this amazing country," he said.

During coffee after dinner, Naomi rose from the table and walked out onto the verandah, followed soon after by Marcus. As they leant on the railing, looking at the water rippling in the moonlight, Marcus asked about her life in Darwin.

"I work in my father's sailing supplies and boat brokerage business in Darwin and live with him at the family home in Callum Bay. My mother and father separated a few years ago. She now lives in Brisbane."

"Do you have any brothers or sisters?"

"Just an older brother who also lives in Brisbane. What about you?"

"My mother and father separated when I was only eight. He married again and I now have a lovely half-sister who lives at Gratton Grange and goes to high school in New Orleans."

"Marcus, I am pleased you will be visiting Darwin again next year. If you were not returning home tomorrow, you could have attended my birthday party next Friday night."

"Oh, I would love to have done that. How old will you be?"

"Twenty."

"I will make sure I am here for your twenty-first. Can I give you a kiss for your twentieth?"

"Please do."

At the dinner table Alex, looking at Jack, commented casually: "That looks like a nice friendship developing."

"Yes, I noticed that too."

CHAPTER 32

O n the flight home from Australia, Brendon told Marcus how much he was missing Louise and that he could hardly wait to see her again.

"Mate, she is a really attractive girl. More than that, she is intelligent and caring. But good luck dealing with her father as you move along with your relationship with his daughter."

"I'm very aware of that. I just need to keep in mind that while he is a tough operator, he seems to be quite fair in dealing with people once he checks them out. I love his daughter and I have a lot of respect for her father."

A couple of days after arriving home, Brendon was provided with a small power boat for the day from his father's boat hire business and took Louise for a picnic on the lake.

He could not keep his eyes off her as she climbed into the boat in a pair of tight shorts and a halter top. They motored for a while until they found a suitably secluded narrow inlet and ran the boat up onto a small beach.

Louise spread a colorful hand-woven rug made by a local Indigenous American Indian woman she knew. They settled into a relaxed lunch of smoked salmon wraps stuffed with soft cheese and avocado.

Fish were jumping in the water, birds were twittering in the trees, and there was scraping in the undergrowth. As he rubbed sunscreen into her back, he kept looking at the way her top was tied. Slowly he undid it. There was a low murmur from her as he slid it off.

Soon, they lay naked on the rug, completely enveloped in their own universe. The birds and the fish were silent. There was no breeze, only the soft lap of the water on the sandy shore.

After a while activity around them came back to life – the birds were chirping. Louise suggested they were conveying comments to each other about the love they had just witnessed.

A spider dropped down on a thin web line from a tree above. Brendon went to kill it but was stopped by Louise. He was told to take it to a bush nearby, which he gingerly did, after catching it in a glass.

"That spider is a part of our magic day. It deserves to live," she said emphatically.

A large multi-colored butterfly landed at the edge of the rug. "Look at this. I love this place and I love you for bringing me here."

"Our love has changed my perspective of life so much. You have opened my eyes to a wider and bright horizon," he said.

A pelican floated past. Then sailed back again for a closer view. Looking at them, and then at the picnic basket, it waddled up the beach and stopped, its huge mouth open. Brendon threw a piece of salmon wrapped in a lettuce leaf. Gulping it down, Pele', as Louise immediately named it, turned, dipped its head, and sailed majestically away.

"What a beautiful bird. I continue to be amazed at the abundance of incredible creatures around this part of the world," she said.

"You would also be amazed at what we saw in Australia. You should come there with Marcus and I when we return next year."

Brendon's father Gerard greeted them at the wharf and helped secure the boat. He noticed a glow about the couple and that they could not keep their hands off each other.

Brendon and Louise were now in their final year studying commerce at Southport. Not only was he putting greater effort into his studies but there was also an increasing concern about what he would do after graduation. In addition, there was an immediate need to earn some money. He decided to phone Louise's father Rick about some casual work in the construction industry.

"Hi Brendon, I've been hearing all about your trip to Australia from Louise. I am glad you called. We have a major project building a new school for a suburb in New Orleans and could use some additional labor. The hours can be flexible to suit your study requirements. I will talk to Ken, the site manager, and get him to contact you."

The following week Brendon met on site with Ken who kitted him out with safety gear including hard hat, gloves and safety googles before showing him around the site and arranging for him to join a team laying bricks. Ken told him that Rick wanted him to gain experience in various areas of construction such as plastering, carpentry, roofing, and construction of water supply and sewerage systems. They agreed that he would work a full day each Thursday as well as each Saturday morning.

Over a coffee at the university with Louise and Marcus, Brendon said he had discovered some muscles that he did not know existed.

"The first couple of days I was aching all over my body, but I certainly slept really well. Would you believe, I am now starting to enjoy the work. Ken has also got me into helping with forward planning for the remaining stages of the project."

"It's just as well that you were already quite fit, otherwise the career of Brendon the laborer could have been quite brief. Good on you for having a go and hanging in there," said Marcus.

Louise took Brendon's hand. "My father is impressed with the way that you are applying yourself to work in the construction industry. I am so proud of you, even if it does mean that I may no longer be the heir apparent."

"Louise, maybe you and I might even become a team in the construction industry."

"Really? Gee, I've never thought about that," she said, looking at Marcus, who smiled without comment.

At the end of their last academic year at Southport, Brendon and Louise were relieved and thrilled to learn that they were to be admitted to the Degree of Bachelor of Commerce.

The graduation ceremony was held in the great hall of the university and those in attendance included their families and friends. Although they had talked on the phone, it was the first time that their proud fathers, Rick and Gerard, had met each other.

Shaking hands, Gerard thanked Rick for the work opportunities he was providing for Brendon. To one side, they talked about the future for the new graduates.

"Rick, it is great to meet you and your family at last, and as for Brendon, Nora and I cannot believe the way his character has developed over the last twelve months or so. I think the relationship between he and Louise is an important part of that."

"Lorie and I are pleased about that relationship. In the part-time work he is doing with my company, Brendon is obviously a quick learner and showing a lot of initiative. Now that they have both graduated, I am thinking about offering them full-time employment with Mangan Construction. Do you have any views about that?"

"He has more than once indicated to me that he very much enjoys working in the construction industry and seems to have developed a good operational relationship with Ken, your site manager. I have always thought he might one day take over management of my family's boat hire business. However, while he is an accomplished sailor, the way things are evolving, I do not think that is where his interest or future lies. I suspect he would jump at your offer, and he would have my full support."

They shook hands again. At Gerard's suggestion, both families agreed to move on to Sirico's for lunch.

The next day as his phone rang, Brendon leapt to answer.

"Just ringing to offer you a job as assistant to Ken in finalizing the school construction project. Louise has agreed to take up a position as my assistant to gain some knowledge in managing the overall operations of Mangan Construction. When the school project is completed in a couple of months, I would like you both to work with me for some time. What do you think of my proposal?"

"Rick, I can't wait to start."

"OK, report to Ken at 8.00 AM on Monday."

This was a major watershed moment in Brendon's life. 'If I do not make a success of this opportunity, what will I then do', he wondered. As much as his relationship with his father had improved over recent times, he did not really want to work in the family business. He wished to be more independent and find his own way in the world. Also, if he failed with Mangan Construction, what sort of an impact could that have on his blossoming relationship with Louise? Feeling there was a lot at stake, for the first time he felt some apprehension about how the future might unfold. There was a lack of confidence entering his thoughts with some doubt about his own ability.

He believed that Marcus was the only person he could talk to about such a matter. He rang and told him about the arrangement to take up a position as Ken's assistant site manager.

"Buddy, can we meet for a coffee at Clarice's café on Bourbon Street this afternoon?

"Sure, is everything OK?

"Yep, just would like to talk through with you some thoughts I have about my future. I'll see you there at 5.00 PM."

Walking down Bourbon Street to Clarice's, Marcus thought about what might be on his friend's mind. His tone of voice indicated that he was not his normal upbeat self. Was there a problem with Louise, perhaps with Rick, or some other concern?

He found him seated towards the back of the café at a quiet table tucked away in a corner. They greeted each other and ordered two long-black coffees.

Marcus listened intently as Brendon outlined his lack of confidence and nervousness prior to taking up the new position. He thought back to the brash self-opinionated young man he met on his first day at university compared to the quite different friend who was now sitting across from him. He did not see this change as a display of any type of weakness, but rather a pause in the progress of his maturity, which was developing at a quick pace.

In offering his views, Marcus would strive to help Brendon achieve clarity in his confused thinking by providing some direction to restore his confidence.

"Buddy, it's your first full-time job after years of full-time study where you did not really have to think much about such things until now. It's only natural that you will feel some apprehension. I'm sure I will feel the same when I start my first full-time job. A big benefit in this situation for you is that you have already worked part-time with Ken, and I doubt you would have been appointed by Rick without Ken's support. He is obviously impressed with the work you have already done on the school project. You are now simply stepping up a level to a position with more responsibility. I'm sure Ken will continue to be very supportive. Do not hesitate to ask him questions as you go along and tap into his operational knowledge. Also, you are now entering a work situation when there could be opportunities to apply things you have learnt during your commerce studies at university. You should consciously look to identify those opportunities. Perhaps you could also think about maintaining contact with your former athletics coach and commerce lecturer, Andre Bellinger, who I know has a high opinion of you and your potential. That could prove to be a win/win friendship, with him giving you advice and updates on the latest developments in the field of commerce, and you providing him with information on your experiences in the construction industry that he could utilize in his lectures. You have plenty of ability. Be positive and embrace the opportunity you have been given."

"Everything you say makes a lot of sense. I so admire your thoughtful level-headed advice in such matters. That's why I rang and asked you to meet me here today. I now feel more relaxed. There is a clearer way ahead and an exciting challenge, rather than worrying about a non-existent looming threat. I will definitely maintain contact with Andre."

As they walked from the café Marcus put his arm around the shoulders of a happier Brendon Lefont.

CHAPTER 33

Marcus, now in his final year at Southport, was achieving outstanding grades in his agricultural science course. It was time to put some serious thought into what he would do after graduation. He decided to arrange a meeting at the Louisiana Agriculture Center.

On arrival he was greeted by the director of the laboratories, Dr Michael Strahan, who said he was already aware of Marcus and his impressive academic performance at Southport.

"We have a close working relationship with the university and have been tracking your progress. We planned to contact you soon, but you got in first," laughed Dr Strahan.

"Thank you for your interest in me. I am very keen to pursue a career in plant pathology, which is the main area that I have been studying at Southport."

"I would think that your family at Gratton Grange would be supportive of your focus in that area. Have you also considered entomology, which is another area where we are doing a lot of advanced research?"

"Gratton Grange has a substantial apiary, but I have found that I am more comfortable dealing with plants than insects."

"I can relate to that – my qualifications are in plant pathology. We have vacancies in both areas, which is why I mentioned entomology. But I must admit that I love Gratton Grange honey. I understand that last year you toured our research laboratories with a group from the university. Would you like to again tour the plant pathology division and talk to some of the scientists there?"

"That would be great. It would give me a good insight into how the division operates and the main areas of current research."

During the tour he was introduced to several plant pathologists who were undertaking a wide variety of research including the development of virus resistant citrus, grape vines, cotton, and various vegetables. The operation of some new electron microscopes was explained, and he was excited to be given the opportunity to view some of the latest research through a powerful lens. Marcus was also taken to view field trials of newly developed plant varieties on land which the center had recently purchased near Cranton.

On return to Dr Strahan's office, he was asked if he would like to join the center after graduation from Southport.

"Thank you so much for the offer. You have an impressive team here and some excellent work is obviously being done. I would love the opportunity to be a member of your team."

"Great. I will provide you with a letter confirming our offer and will look forward to welcoming you aboard after graduation."

Leaving the center, Marcus felt immense excitement together with a sense of relief as he phoned his father. They arranged to meet at Sirico's for a celebratory drink.

Some two months later he caught up with Brendon and noted that he was dressed in what one might call 'smart casual'.

"G'day mate," Marcus said in good Aussie speak. "You are looking well, just like an upwardly mobile young businessman should."

"Thanks. Construction of the new school is completed. I am now really enjoying working alongside Rick and Louise to gain a broad-picture view of the construction industry. There are so many aspects to operating in the industry. Every day is interesting and sometimes quite challenging. Thanks once again for your help in boosting my confidence when I started working as Ken's assistant on the school project. What about you? The grapevine is working overtime about your job offer. Congratulations. Does Naomi know about this?"

"Why do you ask that?"

"Come on, you can't fool me. You looked quite sorrowful in the plane on the way back from Australia. Like a man who had just lost a good friend."

"For your information, although I only met her briefly, she is like a good friend. We are in regular contact. She is looking forward to us staying at Callum Bay on our return to Darwin for the regatta."

"Marcus, Louise is also keen to go on the trip. She asked Rick if it would be OK for us to take a couple of weeks leave during the upcoming summer. He responded that he would do his best to keep the company afloat for that long without our assistance. Just another example of Rick's offbeat sense of humor - he is a good guy. We are developing a strong working relationship."

"You and I are lucky that we have found our career niche early in life. I will let Naomi know that Louise will be travelling with us to Darwin."

CHAPTER 34

L ouise, who had never been overseas before, was enormously excited and a little nervous as they waited in Los Angeles for the long connecting Qantas flight to Australia.

Finally arriving at Darwin airport, they were greeted by Alex and Naomi and bundled with their luggage into an Australian built Ford Territory. Louise said she had no idea that the 'Land Down Under' was so far away from New Orleans and that she felt quite weary after the long-haul trip.

"You can all freshen up and get some rest before dinner," said Alex, which brought a big smile from Louise.

"It is such a lovely warm sunny day. I would like to freshen up with a swim if that is OK," said Marcus looking at Naomi as they arrived in Callum Bay.

"We have a nice swimming pool, so you are most welcome to do that. I will jump in with you," responded a beaming Naomi.

An impressive double story all-white rendered solid brick residence came into view. Alex explained it had strong reinforcement to withstand destructive winds that were not uncommon in Darwin during the monsoon season. The house looked down onto a swimming pool with spa bath. A freshly mown lawn sloped to a private jetty where a sleek cabin cruiser was moored.

While Brendon and Louise had a shower and then rested in their room, Marcus put his bag in his allocated room, pulled on some board shorts and headed to the pool. He had only swum a couple of lengths when Naomi appeared in a skimpy yellow bikini.

"Hello. You are an excellent swimmer. Have you swum competitively?"

"I am captain of the swimming team at university," he said, trying to be as modest as possible. "I must say you look stunning in that bikini."

"Thank you. I try to keep fit through tennis, some golf, and the occasional trip to the gym. I also love horse riding, not that it really helps a lot with keeping fit. But being fit certainly helps in dealing with a spirited horse."

Without further delay, she dived in and came up next to him, grabbed his arm, kissed him, and said: "Welcome to Callum Bay, it's so good to see you again, at last."

After a while they climbed out of the pool and rested on lounges under an umbrella before Alex appeared and announced he had bought some large lobsters from the local seafood shop for dinner, as well as oysters.

"That sounds perfect for dinner on a warm night," said Marcus. "I have a bottle of Gratton Grange Blanc de Bois in my bag which would go well with seafood."

"Why don't you go get it and put it in one of the fridges in the kitchen," said a keenly interested Alex.

After a shower and changing into fresh clothes, Marcus wandered onto the deck next to the pool to find Brendon and Alex chatting about the regatta next weekend.

"Where are the girls?"

"Well, there is a lot of chatter and laughter in the kitchen, but I think they are making a salad. At least I hope they are," mumbled Alex.

Soon after, the girls appeared and set five places at the round table and then returned bearing a large platter with halved lobsters, a huge bowl of garden salad, and five trays, each containing a dozen natural oysters. Alex disappeared inside and returned with glasses and the wine that Marcus had brought.

"Here's to the return of the two American adventurers, plus one this time, and to our success at the regatta in a couple of days. I think we should do well so long as our devious club commodore behaves himself," chuckled Alex, as if almost hoping that might not be the case.

The next day Alex and the boys drove to the yacht club to ready *Sunburst* for the upcoming events. The girls decided to spend the morning at the pool and then have lunch at a café on the Callum Bay boardwalk overlooking the marina. Over lunch Naomi told Louise about her love of horse riding. She suggested that while the blokes were sailing, they might spend some time on a cattle station just over an hour's drive from Darwin.

"But I have never ridden a horse in my life," exclaimed Louise.

"There is always a first time. You will be provided with a quiet well-behaved mare and given expert instruction. Over a couple of days, you could even learn to crack a whip, muster cattle, and help in cattle tagging. Trust me Louise, you will have a great time."

"Just the thought of this is sending shivers down my spine, but it would certainly be quite an adventure and a huge challenge. I am prepared to give it a go."

"Great. I will arrange a fully equipped cabin for us. We will be there by mid-afternoon."

On the morning of the regatta, Alex and the boys were on *Sunburst* early to meet with Burnie plus two experienced crew who regularly sailed on the boat. Alex briefed the crew about the expected conditions, the course, and tactics in the prevailing moderate south easterly wind.

Sunburst was entered in a handicap race on both the Saturday and Sunday. On the first day it took some time for Brendon and Marcus to settle into Alex's stringent requirements and become part of a cohesive unit. But as the race progressed, the yacht performed better in the fresher conditions and completed the course a creditable sixth out of 22 entrants.

On the Sunday, *Sunburst* got away to a better start and the crew were working well as a team following some discussion over dinner the previous night. The race plan was executed almost perfectly except for a brief period when they were becalmed off the Vernon Islands. As they approached the half-way marker the commodore's boat was sighted less than a nautical mile to windward. Alex yelled excitedly for a quick tack to pick up speed for the run home.

Soon after rounding the marker a sudden strong squall came through. Alex ordered the spinnaker to be dropped and the mainsail to be reefed. The squall did not continue for long, and Alex was again keen to increase speed.

"Burnie, give the tiller to me. Go to the mainsail, remove the reef, and get that spinnaker up again. We will give her all we can to keep that pesky commodore back there where he belongs."

CHAPTER 35

A rriving at the cattle station, Naomi introduced Louise to Larry, an indigenous middle-aged man who had grown up there, had worked as a station hand and horse breaker, and was now operations manager of the property.

After settling into a comfortable cabin, complete with cooking facilities, they sat for a while with a glass of cool water on the verandah looking across to a paddock that contained several horses. Before long, a beautiful chestnut galloped up to the fence, looked at them, threw its head back and snorted loudly.

"That's an impressive looking horse, what is its name?" asked Louise.

"Her name is Lady, but she sure is no lady. She is my favorite horse though. We have a kind of love-hate relationship. The first time I rode her she reared violently and when that did not dislodge me, she tried a couple of pig roots, completely without warning. On another occasion I was riding her along quite happily near some trees with low hanging branches when suddenly she veered under a branch and tried to drag me out of the saddle. It was quite a scary moment – I could have been decapitated. It became a contest to see who would give in first, but I was determined not to let her win."

"You still ride her after all that?"

"Oh yes. We have become friends in a strange sort of way. Some days she can be quite placid and at other times a bit mean and unpredictable. Mostly, I can pick her mood. If she turns her head, snorts, and shows the whites of her eyes I know that trouble could be brewing. When she does that, I get even more determined to saddle her up, just to reinforce who is boss. She has pretty much got the message by now."

"How incredible. Is my horse one of those in this paddock?"

"Yours will be Marnie, the little bay over there in the corner who is now making her way over for a closer look at us. Let's go and say hello to her."

Late in the afternoon Naomi saddled Lady, tied her to a rail, and then helped Louise saddle Marnie. She then tied a rope to Marnie's bridle so that she could lead her behind Lady for a few circuits of the paddock to help Louise become accustomed to being on horseback. Then she removed the lead and for the first time in her life a nervous Louise was in control of a horse, trotting along beside Naomi.

As they removed the saddles Larry walked over with some apples, steaks, and sausages.

"The apples are for your trusty steeds and the meat is for your barbeque dinner tonight. Tomorrow we will muster some young cattle for tagging."

"Thanks Larry, see you then," Naomi said, turning to Louise. "You should watch as I feed this apple to Lady. Notice that I am holding it on the flat palm of my hand as I offer it to her. Never do this with your fingers extended grasping the apple, otherwise they could be consumed together with the apple. Here, offer this one to Marnie."

"Oh, look how she nibbles rather than grabbing it like Lady. I like this horse. See how she is munching away now with her eyes closed – obviously enjoying it."

"You and Marnie are now friends for life. Lady would never eat an apple with her eyes closed. She likes to always be able to see what is going on around her."

Back on the verandah they relaxed with a bottle of full-bodied Barossa Valley Shiras while the steaks and sausages sizzled.

"How do you feel after your first riding experience?"

"Much more relaxed than when I started. Apart from a sore behind, I am feeling quite exhilarated. I am a bit worried about going on the cattle muster tomorrow though."

"You will be fine. Marnie is easy to handle and most of the work will be done by the dogs. Basically, we just provide the direction. Marnie is a stayer with a big heart and will still be going strong at the end of the day. Lady is more likely to tire due to her frisky nature. We will be rounding up about 50 young cattle and bringing them to holding pens for tagging. You will be in the saddle for a while with just a water bottle plus some nuts and stuff in your saddle bag to nibble on."

Early next morning Larry rode up, tied his horse to a hitching rail in front of the cabin, and watched while the girls saddled their horses and led them over.

"G'day girls. Louise, here is a stock whip. You will not be expected to use it today, but its best that you know how to."

With that, he swung the whip and unleashed a loud crack like a shot from a gun that made Louise flinch. After several tries, she managed to produce a good result which drew praise from her instructor and clapping from Naomi.

They set off with two kelpie dogs, one red and the other black, scampering around them until Larry whistled the red one to jump up behind him. Naomi motioned to the other to do the same, much to Louise's amazement, and a toss of the head from Lady.

After riding for some time, they came across a bunch of grazing cattle. Then, a little further on, a larger bunch which they rounded up to join the others. They moved the whole herd along in the general direction of the homestead and holding yards.

Arriving back, they herded the cattle into the yards. The horses were freed for a drink and to feed in the home paddock.

The young cattle were progressively moved through a gate from the holding yards down a narrow race to a head gate designed to hold the head steady, then fitted with an identity tag and released into a holding paddock. A station hand showed Louise how to operate the head gate and how to use a tag applicator.

The following day, after a hearty breakfast cooked on the barbeque, the girls again saddled the horses and rode to a large dam a short ride from the homestead. Naomi checked the water supply and valves at several stock troughs for Larry before they headed back.

After lunch it was time to return to Darwin to greet Alex, Marcus and Brendon at the yacht club following the last race of the regatta. As they fed apples to the horses Louise said how much she had enjoyed the weekend.

"I am going to miss Marnie very much. She has such a lovely calm disposition and I have already grown attached to her," she said, stroking the horse's nose over the fence.

"Perhaps you can get a horse for yourself when you return home."

"That might be possible. Maybe I could talk to Marcus and do a deal about keeping it at Gratton Grange."

There was a huge gathering at the club to welcome the fleet home. They were spread out over about two nautical miles with *Sunburst* coming in fourth on corrected time followed closely by the commodore's boat.

Much cheering and hugging took place as the boats arrived. Naomi and Louise had already secured a table and arranged chilled champagne in ice buckets together with a large platter of finger food. As *Sunburst* docked, the girls helped tie her off as the guys leapt onto the wharf.

Giving Brendon a huge hug, Louise noticed he was sunburnt.

"Brendon, did you use the sunscreen that I gave you?"

"Yes, but wind burn got to me. Don't worry, I'm all fired up for a big night of celebrations. We beat the commodore across the line," he said with obvious glee, encouraged by comments from Alex.

The commodore came up to their table, was handed a glass of champagne, and complimented Alex on *Sunburst's* performance.

"That wasn't the sound of a motor that I heard while we were becalmed off the Vernon Islands," said Alex with a sly grin.

"I had to do something to try and catch you, but don't tell anyone," said the commodore, continuing the banter. "You and your crew sailed a great race."

CHAPTER 36

While Naomi was at work, Louise, Brendon, and Marcus packed a lot into the following days including a guided tour of Litchfield National Park where they swum under waterfalls and viewed beautiful indigenous art in caves that was thousands of years old. Following a lot of encouragement from Brendon, Louise even tried some bush tucker.

The tour also provided Louise with an opportunity to tell Marcus about the great experience she had on the cattle station.

"Marcus, I fell in love with this beautiful horse called Marnie. Could you ask Jack and Salina if they might allow me to agist a horse at Gratton Grange so that I can enjoy riding again."

"I will be happy to do that Louise. There is a piece of land near Sam's house that would be perfect. I have a feeling that Salina could be an enthusiastic supporter of your request. You might even have a new riding partner."

Next Saturday was Naomi's 21st birthday and a big party had been arranged at her home in Callum Bay. A large marque was erected on the lawn that contained a bar and long trestle tables laden with food. Multi-colored fairy lights twinkled from trees and across a stage where a band played disco dance music.

Over 100 people had been invited including several from the yacht club, and the clubs where Naomi played tennis and golf. It was a joyous occasion with lots of laughter, people showing off their best dance moves, and others splashing around in the pool. Louise was delighted to see Larry there, drinking a beer with Marcus and Brendon, and a couple of hands from the cattle station.

Around midnight Alex stepped onto the stage and with the assistance of a loud drum roll, called for some quiet and proceeded to deliver a speech thanking everyone for attending and helping Naomi celebrate her 21st. birthday. He spoke for a while about how much he loved his daughter and how she had developed into a beautiful and talented young lady. Glasses were topped up and three cheers rang out as Naomi was toasted and the band sprang back to life.

Brendon and Louise had been given their own room at one end of the house, and Marcus was provided with a room overlooking the water where Alex's cabin cruiser rested at the jetty.

After the festivities finally came to an end, Marcus was in his room and about to climb into bed when his phone rang.

"Would you like a nightcap down here on the boat?" whispered Naomi as if worried she might be overheard.

"Yes, I'll be right down."

Upstairs, Alex walked along the passage to say goodnight to Naomi, but she was not there.

Looking out of his bedroom window he noticed a light on in the cabin of his boat.

'I just hope she hasn't forgotten to take the pill' he thought, collapsing into bed.

But he had trouble sleeping and an hour later looked out through the parted drapes. All was quiet in the moonlight, except the occasional splash of the incoming tide on the jetty pilons. The light on the boat had gone out. He wished them well.

At the airport waiting to board a plane and start the long journey home, Marcus took Naomi aside.

"You should come to New Orleans for my graduation. In addition to the probable agistment of a horse for Louise, I plan to suggest to Salina that Gratton Grange buys a couple of horses. We could go riding together and sailing. You could sample Cajun food, and you and I could ride on a paddle steamer up the Mississippi to Baton Rouge listening to some of the best music in the world."

"Darling, I will be there. I just wish I could go with you right now."

When Marcus asked Salina about introducing horses to Gratton Grange she was immediately enthusiastic. Her face lit up, like she was already dreaming about being involved in a new exciting experience.

"What a great idea. I would love to learn to ride, and I cannot wait to meet Naomi. She sounds like a very switched on and capable young lady. I will talk to Sam about a dedicated paddock. It will have nice white railing fences, good pasture, a water trough, and some stables will be constructed. There are lots of trails that extend north, even beyond Cranton, where we can ride and explore the countryside."

After consultation with Sam, work started on fencing a piece of land near Sam's house that was formerly part of Cooper's cotton plantation.

Sam took Salina, Louise, and Marcus to meet a friend who operated a property near Cranton where retired racehorses were offered for sale. The manager explained that the aim was to provide the horses with a pleasant retirement and save them from the knackery.

Marcus was interested in an impressive chestnut mare for Naomi that Louise told him looked like Lady back in Australia.

"There is quite a similarity in looks to Lady, but a big difference in behavior. This horse is more placid, but quite alert, and more like a lady should be," said Louise.

"I will buy this 'ladylike' horse for Naomi," declared Marcus.

Louise selected a beautiful six-year-old bay mare named La Bella that reminded her of Marnie, while Salina went for a striking black mare called Black Diamond which she was told had won many races in its prime.

Arrangements were made to transport the horses to Gratton Grange at the end of the month when facilities to accommodate them would be completed. Saddles and bridles would be provided as part of the deal.

Travelling back to Gratton Grange with Sam, Salina said she had not thought before what happened to racehorses at the end of their racing career.

"I enjoyed watching the racing at the Kentucky Derby and won some money, but never thought about this at all. I am so pleased, Marcus and Louise, that you went to Australia and came back with this great idea. We have now saved the lives of three beautiful horses."

Marcus phoned Naomi to tell her about the horse that he had bought for her and sent a photo.

"Oh Marcus, thank you so much, she looks a lot like Lady. What is her name?"

"Her registered name is Chiquita, but you may wish to change that."

"No. It is a lovely name. She should keep it, and I cannot wait to meet and ride her. I am counting off the days on my calendar until I see you again."

When a weary Naomi finally arrived at the New Orleans airport she was met by Marcus. They held each other tightly for so long that an elderly lady nearby suggested to her husband that it must have been some time since they had seen each other.

"Isn't young love wonderful," she said wistfully.

At Gratton Grange Salina told Naomi how much she had looked forward to meeting her as she showed her to an upstairs room in the manor house over-looking the Mississippi River.

"You should get some rest after your long journey and then, before dinner, I will introduce you to Chiquita," Salina suggested.

"I can't wait, can I meet her now?"

"Of course, let's go."

As they approached the paddock Salina's horse Black Diamond galloped up to the fence followed at a slower pace by the other two. Naomi called out to Chiquita who came tentatively forward to within a few feet of the fence. She held out her hand, but the horse would not come any further, so she climbed through the rails and walked slowly towards her. Talking softly and calling her name, she patted Chiquita's neck. Gradually the horse turned its head and touched her shoulder with its nose.

"Salina, I think she knows that I am a friend of horses, and I think she likes me."

"I'm sure she does. Stay there for a moment while I take a photo for you to send to your father and your friend Larry. They will be interested to see you with your new horse."

The next day Louise arrived. Although she was still in a learning phase herself, she had been able to assist Salina with the basics of saddling and riding a horse within the confines of the paddock. Naomi was impressed with the progress that Salina had already made.

The girls saddled the horses and rode to a trail heading north around the outskirts of Cranton. They rode along and chatted happily in the sunshine – three confident women on three lovely well-behaved horses. Looking at the elegant posture of Salina in the saddle, Naomi noted how well she related to Black Diamond. She suggested that, with some training, horse and rider could be a successful combination in competitive show events.

"Do you really think so?" laughed Salina. "I must say, this is a magnificent horse. I might just think about that."

"I'm serious. You should."

CHAPTER 38

Salina took Naomi on a tour of the entire Gratton Grange operations. Surprisingly, she showed a keen interest in the apiary and asked if she could assist in maintenance that was required for some of the hives. Kitted out in protective gear, Naomi was fascinated as she witnessed the amazing world in the hives where the bees lived, and she learnt about the important contribution they make to the environment.

"I never took much notice of bees before," she said, peering into a highly active hive. "Look at all these worker bee's buzzing in and out, crawling over each other. Sometimes they even seem to kiss each other. Look over there at that small pond where they are skiing over the top and then settling for a drink on the edge. It seems like an incredibly coordinated and apparently loving community with one objective – to build honeycombs for the queen."

Returning to the manor house they sat down to coffee together with Gratton Grange Honey on toast. Salina explained how the honey business operated including establishment, maintenance, harvesting, packaging, and marketing.

"I love the taste and golden color of this honey, and the design of the packaging. I am not surprised that there is a big demand for it in the marketplace. Have you thought about developing an export market?"

"I am the one who is responsible for the honey business as well as for the vineyard operation, so I am stretched rather thin. But you are right. We need to look at export of both our honey and wine. Tomorrow we will go to Marcus's graduation ceremony at Southport. Do you have a nice dress to wear? I think dresses are the go for such an occasion, including afterwards at lunch which will be at our restaurant."

"I brought a couple of little summer dresses. Let me show you."

"They are lovely. I particularly like the orange-colored one."

"Me too. That is the one I will wear. Orange ochre is a prominent color in the Top End of Australia, where I live. It features in a lot in the beautiful artwork of our aborigines."

Following the graduation ceremony, a large crowd gathered for lunch at Gratton Grange Estate restaurant which was closed for the private event. Marcus's mother and grandparents from New York were there as well as Louise and Brendon and their respective parents, plus Sam and Belinda, Joey and Beth, and friends from the university and yacht club. Naomi looked radiant in her orange ochre dress as she nestled next to Marcus at the official table which included Salina and Jack. Eloise was also at the table. She had developed into a beautiful and charming young lady who was studying music and learning to play the violin in New York.

Jessica, in charge of the busy kitchen, had earlier prepared the three-course menu and accompanying wine list with Salina. Prior to serving of the main course, Jack delivered an emotional speech about how proud he was of his son's achievements and the bright future that he was sure lay ahead for him.

He also paid tribute to his former wife and Marcus's mother Laura, acknowledging the outstanding part she had played in his upbringing.

"Although I did my best to assist financially, it would not have been easy for you at times Laura. You are to be congratulated for the excellent role that you have played," he said.

Laura, seated on the other side of Marcus, smiled, and nodded in appreciation of Jack's comments.

Two days before Naomi was due to return to Darwin, she met Marcus for lunch at Sirico's.

"I can't believe how quickly the days have gone since I arrived in New Orleans two weeks ago. I love it here and have had such a wonderful time meeting your family and friends. I am going to miss you so much and don't know how I will survive back home without you," she said, staring at him wide eyed with a forlorn expression.

"I love you. We must agree on a plan," responded Marcus. "Why don't you move here permanently? We could rent nice accommodation in New Orleans. I will be starting work as an agricultural scientist soon and I understand that the yacht club is looking for an executive assistant to the general manager. That could be perfect for you with your experience working in your father's boat business."

Grabbing his hand over the table, she burst into tears. "I love you too. That is what we will do."

"Good. I will fly back to Darwin with you. We will sit down with your father and discuss our plans with him. He is a good man. I am sure he will understand."

A waitress came up to their table and asked if everything was OK.

"Yes, thank you. I am crying with happiness," Naomi managed to say. "I will be moving from Australia to live here."

"Welcome to The Big Easy. Marcus, you are a lucky man."

Having been forewarned by Naomi during a phone conversation that Marcus would be accompanying her on the flight back to Darwin, Alex was waiting for them at the airport as the plane landed.

He sensed that an important discussion lay ahead and suggested that they drive straight to his home followed by lunch at the Callum Bay marina.

Shifting nervously in his chair beside Alex's pool, Marcus outlined to him the plan for Naomi to move to New Orleans. He told him that they were very much in love and said he hoped that he would understand.

"Marcus, I am not at all surprised. I have watched with interest the development of your strong relationship with Naomi. I will miss her enormously, but I know she will be happy with you. She goes with my blessing, and I wish you both well."

Naomi stood, moved across to her father, sat on his knee and kissed him.

"Alex, thank you so much for your support. It is invaluable to us," said Marcus. "You should come and visit us soon in New Orleans. Also, you should stay for a few days at Gratton Grange. My father will be delighted to see you again."

"I will definitely do that, and maybe go sailing with you and Brendon. I have only been to the US once before – just to Los Angeles for a few days. This adventure that you two are embarking on could open-up a whole new world of travel for me. I am already getting excited."

"Dad, during the flight here Marcus and I agreed to come back to Darwin for the next regatta, perhaps with Brendon and Louise. She and I could catch up with Larry and go riding again. Hopefully, Lady will be pleased to see me."

Before returning to New Orleans, Naomi spent several days rearranging her affairs including paying any outstanding bills, cancelling numerous accounts, and becoming a social member instead of a full member of the tennis and golf clubs. New arrangements would have to be made for things such as banking, health insurance, dentist, a new driver's license, and a Green Card would be needed for employment in the US. She asked her father to sell her small SUV and send her the proceeds. When they returned to visit from time-to-time they would hire a vehicle.

There was a need to inform all her friends about what was happening. This was going to be a full-on lifestyle transformation. Quite nervous but also excited, she could not have undertaken such a venture unless she was deeply in love and trusted Marcus implicitly.

Naomi's main concern about leaving Darwin was the impact it would have on her father. It was several years since her mother had left and taken her brother with her to live in Brisbane. During those years she and her father had grown very close. Now he would not only be left in the big house by himself, but he would also have to find someone else to assist in running the business. As she made final arrangements to leave, a feeling of sadness and some guilt crept over her. She was torn between her love for Marcus and concern for her father.

While Marcus was having a swim in the pool, Alex walked past her room and heard her sobbing. He looked in, calling her name. She emerged from a walk-in robe where she was packing clothes into a large travel bag.

"Hello Dad, come in. Sorry I am expressing my feelings so audibly on this momentous occasion. I thought I would deal with my move from Darwin to the US much calmer than this."

Alex held her close and then sat with her on the side of the bed.

"Darling, what is worrying you?

Drying her eyes, she struggled to tell him: "Dad, it is you. I am worried that I have put my own interests first. I am walking away from you and creating a problem for you in running your business. I feel like a very selfish person."

"You are not and never have been selfish. You have come to a time in your life that you must follow your heart. I would be very disappointed if I were the reason for you not doing that. It is obvious that you love Marcus and that he loves you. As for me, I have many friends in Darwin, plus a business that I enjoy operating and which keeps me busy. It may seem such a long distance from New Orleans to here, but really, it is only a couple of plane rides away. We should make a pact that we will see each other regularly, perhaps once a year or so. Either I will travel to New Orleans for a visit, or you will come here, and of course we can talk on the phone at any time."

"Oh yes, I like that arrangement. You always have good ideas to fix difficult situations."

Marcus appeared in the doorway with a towel draped around him.

"Hi mate, Naomi and I have just been discussing her concern about deserting me. I have told her that although I will miss her being around every day, I have plenty of friends here and will be OK."

Alex told Marcus about their plan to maintain contact.

"Alex, I had already been thinking about the need to maintain regular contact and can fully understand Naomi's emotions at a time like this. I love coming to Darwin and will be more than happy to accompany her and catch up with you and the boys at the yacht club."

"I am relieved and much happier now. You are the two most important people in my life. I love you both so much," Naomi said, wiping away another tear.

Although Naomi was now more relaxed, a warning sign appeared for Marcus which he was quick to recognize. She would need strong support when they arrived back in the US to help find her feet and settle into a new life. Alex would play his part by maintaining regular contact.

As they settled into their seats on the plane at Darwin airport, a comment from Naomi confirmed for Marcus that the gravity of her move to the US continued to occupy her mind.

"Marcus, we are so lucky that long distance overseas travel is now mostly by aircraft rather than by ship. In earlier days, a trip such as this would have taken ages to do by sea and been much more difficult for us."

"Yes darling, we can now travel easily wherever and whenever we wish."

As the plane left the terminal and taxied for take-off, she held Marcus' hand tightly and waved to Alex who she thought she could see waving to her, but by now she was too far away from the terminal viewing area to be sure.

CHAPTER 39

Arriving back in New Orleans, Marcus and Naomi stayed for a couple of weeks at Gratton Grange before they found a nice terrace house in the Garden District of New Orleans to rent. Marcus commenced work at the Agriculture Centre after introducing Naomi to the general manager of the yacht club. An interview for the vacant executive assistant position was arranged.

Meanwhile, Brendon and Louise had been working closely with Rick to learn the strategies and processes in managing a successful corporation in the construction industry. They had learnt about the importance of attention to detail in the effective management of projects on a day-to-day basis. Working well as a team, they were now also able to identify opportunities, challenges, and likely pitfalls in considering potential new projects.

In his office early one morning, Rick revealed to them that he had been looking at the idea of establishing a subsidiary of Mangan Construction in Cranton.

"Over recent years I have observed a deterioration in the economic and social life of Cranton. There is a significant opportunity to play a lead role in revitalizing the city. I have registered a new company called Cranton Construction and prepared a draft business plan for us to look at. The inner city is looking shabby. It needs some rejuvenating projects including a new commercial and shopping precinct. This could include an attractive city square with lawns, a spectacular water feature and lots of seating where people can relax. A café culture, reflecting Louisiana's French and Spanish heritage, could be developed around the square where people can enjoy indoor and outdoor dining. There is a need to create more employment opportunities in the city, which our initiatives can contribute to, and attract more visitors, including tourists."

"I love the sound of this. It is really exciting," said Louise.

Brendon nodded, flicking through the business plan document. "I like it too, but I feel there is also a need to do something about the lack of new housing at a reasonable price, especially on the outskirts of Cranton. Some of the homes are only fit for demolition."

"Brendon, if you go to the latter pages of the business plan, you will see that Mangan Construction currently owns a significant piece of land in one of the outer areas of the city. I propose to transfer that asset across to the new entity, Cranton Construction, with a view to building a new housing estate on the land. In addition, we could look to purchase several dilapidated properties in the center of the city and submit plans for a redevelopment, around a new city square, to the local council. However, I suspect that will not be an easy process as the council has a growing reputation for obstruction. There are even some rumors of corruption at City Hall."

Rick paused for a moment, and then went on.

"I am concerned about the amount of materials waste in the construction industry, which often goes to landfill. Therefore, I am suggesting that Cranton Recycling be created as a separate division of Cranton Construction. Its role would be to recycle construction materials, especially from demolition works.

"Louise, I am offering you and Brendon the opportunity to become joint managing directors of Cranton Construction and to be share-holders in the company. I will chair the new company's board, of which you both will be members. What do you think of the draft business plan and my proposal?"

Louise rose excitedly and hugged her father while Brendon looked at him incredulously. He could not believe the relaxed way in which he conveyed his big picture plans to them. Here was a man who had once threatened to sue him after a car crash that had severely injured his daughter. Now he was sitting across from him as he offered a huge opportunity to them both. He felt enormous admiration for the character of this man.

"I think the whole concept is brilliant. Thank you so much for your faith in us, and especially your belief and trust in me. Be assured, I will not let you down," said an emotional Brendon, shaking Rick's hand and hugging Louise.

"OK, I will outline our plans at the upcoming board meeting of Mangan Construction and seek agreement to the transfer of land to Cranton Construction. As soon as the proposed arrangements are in place, can I suggest that you find new accommodation in Cranton and move out of your rented unit in Baton Rouge. Lorie and I own a nice relatively new condominium in Cranton over-looking the Mississippi. The lease is about to expire so you could move into that. We will also need to talk about priorities in your new roles, as well as salary packages, which of course will be identical in value."

Rick was pleased with the way the master plan for his business operations and his family's future was working out, although he sometimes wondered whether he was being selfish in his thinking. He also knew that it was crucial to the success of the strategy that he was able to take his family along with him in agreeing the plan, plus Brendon, who was increasingly looking like a possi-ble new addition to the family.

In the process, he had overcome a major potential hurdle that he had earlier identified – how to ensure a fair and acceptable entry to the family's business operations for both Louise and Brendon. They would work side-by-side, on equal terms. The pressure of running a new business would help to provide an indication of their abilities to perform, as well as whether their relationship was likely to remain strong and progress into the future.

Rick had thought at length about the new business arrangements but had only discussed them briefly with his wife Lorie. He realized there were signif-icant risks financially, and there could also be problems in dealing with City Hall about his proposals for the city of Cranton.

He decided to explain the plan in more depth to Lorie and ask for her views about the weight of responsibility he was asking two young people to shoulder.

"Rick, I understand that there are significant risks involved in this huge project, but we have not gotten to the successful position that we are now in without taking risks. I have enormous confidence in your business judgement and especially your ability in risk management. In relation to the involvement of Louise and Brendon in the establishment and ongoing operation of Cranton Construction, as chairman you will be in a good position to oversight and guide those young people. At the same time, you should provide them with the free-dom to take responsibility and develop their own management styles. Louise is a very level-headed young lady with a maturity beyond her years, while from all reports Brendon is highly regarded by Ken as a quick learner and hard worker who enjoys a challenge. I believe the partnership between Louise and

Brendon will work out well. I am also very impressed by the thoughtful and considerate way you have gone about this whole arrangement – it is a credit to you."

A reserved and not usually demonstrative man, Rick reached out and kissed his wife. "Thanks Lorie, your continuing support means an enormous amount to me. I am sure we will make a great success of this project – something that the people of Cranton will be proud of."

CHAPTER 40

Just prior to turning 60 Jack told Salina that he was thinking about retiring as a surgeon.

"I think it might be time for a change of direction in my working life," he explained. "I no longer have the same daily commitment. Also, my hands are not as agile as they need to be as a surgeon due to some recent signs of arthritis."

"I understand darling. Do you have any thoughts about what you might do instead?"

"No, but there is no rush. However, I would like to advise Julian at the clinic and Tom at the hospital as soon as possible about my intention to retire.

A few days after his 60th birthday party at Sirico's Jack received a phone call from Barry Blake, editor of the Cranton Chronicle. Barry said he had heard about Jack's retirement as a surgeon and would like to talk to him about what his plans might be for the future.

"Barry, I will be happy to do that. The Chronicle has been helpful over the years in its coverage of the development of Gratton Grange. I would like to repay that in some way. Why don't you come over for lunch?"

Jack preferred a private lunch, so he asked Jessica to organize a cold seafood platter and salad to be delivered from the Gratton Grange Estate restaurant to the manor house. He also asked Salina if she would like to join them, but she declined, saying she was busy with the apiary and anyway it would be nice for just the two men to have a chat over lunch together.

Barry was a friendly articulate man in his mid-forties with a dry down-to-earth sense of humor. He was born in Cranton, went to school in Cranton, and then majored in English literature at the Southern Louisiana University in New Orleans. After joining the Chronicle as a journalist, he had worked his way up to the position of editor and was now also a part-owner of the newspaper. He was absolutely dedicated to advancing the City of Cranton and its 25,000 people.

It was a warm sunny day as they sat at a table on the upstairs veranda overlooking the river. Jack opened a bottle of Gratton Grange Estate Chardonnay as Jessica delivered lunch.

"What does it feel like to be retired Jack?"

"I must say I feel a little unsettled walking away from a long career as a surgeon, but I think the timing was right. The clinic is functioning well with Julian in charge. We have arranged for a young surgeon from New Haven, recommended by Rebecca Durham, to replace me in the team. I am not sure that getting more involved in the running of Gratton Grange would be a preferable way to go. It could likely have a destabilizing effect on the current arrangements, which are working very well. At this stage I guess I have an open mind about my future activities."

"Well Jack, I have some thoughts about that which you might like to consider. I love Cranton. Its strong in my blood. The city always had a friendly, egalitarian, and embracing society. People did not hesitate to help each other out in difficult times, regardless of your circumstances or, most importantly, the color of your skin. But over recent times I and others around town have noticed an escalating change in the feel and vibrancy of our city. There is a selfishness creeping in which we never saw before, and there is an obvious deterioration in our local economy. Several shops in the main street are now empty, many street surfaces have deteriorated, and our sporting facilities are neglected because they are not used as much anymore by the young people. There is also an increase in crime, especially associated with drugtaking. We are now having trouble staffing our hospitals and clinics because professionals such as doctors and dentists do not want to work and live here. The Chronicle has also been impacted. Our advertising revenue has decreased significantly, and we are being leant on in relation to our editorial content. It is a depressing situation. Something has to be done about it, and quickly."

"Leant on? What do you mean? How and by whom?"

"There is an increase in graft and corruption, starting I believe with influence being wielded from the top in City Hall. Years ago, around the time that you came down from New York to New Orleans to help in the restoration after the hurricane, Pascale Cambolli also drifted in from New York and set up a shop in Cranton. You may remember, it was a small men's-wear shop in the main street which offered up-market fashions not seen before in Cranton. It became popular, especially with the young men around town. Gradually, Cambolli acquired four other shops in the main street and then purchased a few acres on the edge of town where he now lives and grows vegetables. He also proceeded to build a high profile in Cranton which was helped by providing contributions to local charities and sporting clubs."

"Barry, up to now most of my focus had been on the development of Gratton Grange and on the City of New Orleans due to my work at the clinic and hospitals there. However, I am aware of growing concerns about the deteriorating community landscape in Cranton. One can feel and see it just by walking down the main street and I have heard rumors about a corrupt regime at City Hall. The situation seems to have become a lot worse since Cambolli was elected mayor about four years ago."

"The corruption goes a lot deeper than you may think. People have been saying for some time that Cambolli is growing more than vegetables on his farm. There is a belief that the local police turn a blind eye and are on the take. It is common knowledge that the Cranton chief of police, Mick Marshall, is a close friend of Cambolli."

"You are suggesting that Cambolli is growing cannabis amongst the rows of vegetables as a commercial crop?"

"That is the strong rumor that is going around, but we do not know for sure because only Cambolli and the three or four men who work the farm for him have access to the property. It is an operation that is cloaked in secrecy. Some are suggesting it is likely that other drugs are also being produced at the property."

"Good heavens, what a depressing scenario."

"Jack, elections for the council and mayor of Cranton are due in six weeks and nominations close in two weeks. You should consider running for the council and the position of mayor. Currently there are five councilors including the mayor. Two of those councilors almost always vote with Cambolli, which gives the group a majority vote in decision-making. If you were prepared to run, I can provide two prominent people who would run with you on your ticket."

"Who are those people, Barry?"

"One is the manager of the main supermarket in Cranton, Phil Ormond, and the other is Suzette Inglis who owns Cranton Furniture."

"I know them both, they are excellent people. They are also very brave people, going on what you have told me."

"I do not deny that there is some danger in what I am proposing. But I have a good informant in the Cranton Police Department at a senior level, just below Mick Marshall. Also, very much between you and me, the US Drug Enforcement Agency is now taking an interest in what is happening in Cranton. We will have some strong support on our side if we go ahead, as well as, I believe, most of the people of Cranton."

"You have convinced me that there is an urgent need for action to revitalize the city. I think I could play a role in that. Let me talk to Salina and Sam and get back to you."

Soon after Barry left, Jack asked Sam to come over for a chat. He outlined the discussion he had with Barry and sought Sam's comments.

"Jack, a few days ago Barry spoke to me about your retirement from the clinic and whether you might be interested in nominating for the upcoming council elections. I have known Barry for many years. He is an outstanding citizen. We are lucky to have a man of such integrity as editor of the Chronicle. I told him that he should approach you directly and that while the proposal was extremely challenging and even threatening, a leader of strong character is needed to fix the problems in Cranton. I said you might be that person. If you agree to take up the challenge you can be assured of my complete support and assistance in your campaign."

"Thankyou Sam. I am certainly interested, but I need to discuss the proposal with Salina who I think is in the kitchen talking to Beth. Stay here and I will go get her."

Salina listened intently as the two men outlined the proposal. Then she turned to Jack and darkly said: "I do not like this idea at all. I have also heard the rumors about Cambolli and corruption. There are enormous dangers of you directly confronting such a man and his associates. If you campaigned against him, you would at the very least have to insinuate that he is corrupt. These people would have a lot to lose, so you could expect some very fierce opposition. They could go to any lengths, legal or illegal, to stop you. However, if you truly wish to proceed you will have my full support."

"Thank you both so much. When people such as Barry Blake, Phil Ormond, and Suzette Inglis are prepared to stand up and be counted I cannot stand by and do nothing. I now have the time to get involved and that is what I will do. It is a potentially dangerous proposal, but we cannot just ignore what is happening, watch the continuing decline of Cranton, and let Cambolli have his way. I will run without allegiance to any political party."

As she watched Sam leave, Salina was more concerned about the turn of events than she was prepared to admit. She felt a nervousness in the pit of her stomach that she was having difficulty managing. A tremor shot down her spine. Never had she felt like this before. A real sense of impending danger had entered her life and she was extremely worried for the safety of the man she deeply loved.

But her love was unconditional. She had voiced her concerns about the proposal, but it was obvious that Jack really wished to forge ahead. She understood him enough to know that if she opposed his run for mayor, it was almost certain that he would not proceed. But she also knew if that happened, she would never forgive herself for standing in the way of his obvious desire to contest the election. Maybe their relationship would never be quite the same again. Regardless of her concerns, Salina decided to ensure that they would not be displayed. She would summon her courage and walk confidently beside him through the upcoming campaign.

Returning from seeing Sam out, Jack noticed that she looked a little downcast.

"Darling, I know you have serious reservations about this proposed campaign. If you wish me to not proceed, I will withdraw, and love you just as much. Our wonderful relationship is the most important thing to me."

"No, No, No, we will go forward together on this. You will win the election and I will do my very best to support you.

The next day Jack rang Barry and advised that he would run for mayor and that he would be honored to have Phil and Suzette on his ticket for election to the council. He also told Barry that he was concerned about the safety of his team and their respective family's during the election campaign. In view of what Barry had told him about Cambolli's influence at the top of the local police force, he also questioned whether any real police protection could be expected.

"My contact in the Police Department has advised me that he will ensure that significant police presence will be provided at all public events for those running for election," Barry said.

"Thanks Barry, but I think my team is going to need more personal protection than that. I have a friend who I met when working at the hospital in New Orleans who runs a private security business. He is prepared to provide a personal security officer for each member of my team that I will pay for at a reasonable negotiated rate. He will also provide around-the-clock protection at Gratton Grange during the election campaign, and possibly for some time after."

CHAPTER 41

Jack invited Phil and Suzette to a meeting at Gratton Grange that was also attended by Salina and Sam. In addition, Axcelle Johnson was there – a big but genial African American who owned a security agency in New Orleans. He was fully aware of the problems that the people of Cranton were confronted with.

At the meeting, Suzette delivered a spirited introductory outline of the main issues in Cranton and why she had decided to nominate for council and join Jack's team.

"Municipal rates have increased substantially in recent years but there is not a lot to show for it. City Hall accounts have been audited but the audit report for the last accounting period has still not been released. This is a major cause for concern, especially with an election looming. Does City Hall have something to hide?" she asked. "Unemployment and crime are continuing to increase as well as bankruptcy and poverty. There is a need for more affordable new housing as well as an increase in social housing for destitute people."

Jack responded by saying that if his team was elected, they would immediately arrange for an independent audit of City Hall accounts.

"We will up-the-anti on councilors and public officials who can be identified as not discharging their responsibilities in an ethical and efficient way. We will bring to account those who have contributed to the deterioration of the once beautiful and prosperous city of Cranton," he said with a look of steely determination which Salina had not seen before.

"I have prepared a promotional program for our team which, if agreed, we should activate immediately. It includes paid advertising in the Cranton Chronicle and on local radio and TV, plus printing of posters and leaflets promoting our team for broad distribution throughout the city. I will do an interview with Barry which he will publish in the Chronicle and I will also be available for interviews on radio and TV. In the week prior to the election, I propose that we hold a mass meeting in the town hall where I will be the keynote speaker. We will outline the problems facing Cranton, the importance of the council elections, and the need for change. Each member of the team can present their plans for reviving the city, and we can then take questions from the audience."

Over the weeks leading up to the town hall meeting Jack and Salina visited many businesses, asking them to make the leaflets available to their customers and to prominently display the posters. As they walked the streets of the city many people came up with obvious enthusiasm, shook hands, and wished Jack well in his run for mayor.

Jack, who was already quite well known, now became an instant celebrity. He was starting to thrive on the recognition and acknowledgement that seemed to be increasingly coming his way. It was bolstered by a double page editorial in the Chronicle featuring a large photo of him with his arm around a smiling Salina.

Unfortunately, with the promotion behind Jack's team really beginning to take off, it was not long before negative responses started to flow. Some of the posters began to be ripped down, large pick-up trucks from out of town with loud hailers and big placards for Cambolli suddenly appeared. Paid advertising was taken in the local media by his associates.

A concern for safety rose in the community, but at the same time a determination to stand up and be counted, became more apparent. The day of the town hall meeting there was real excitement in the air and a great sense of anticipation. Across the entrance to the hall was a giant banner with the bold message: **VOTE 1 FOR LANSELL'S LIBERATORS.** Many citizens had undertaken to hand out Lansell leaflets in defiance of enormous antagonism and threats from Cambolli associates who looked more like thugs than genuine supporters.

By early evening, the town hall was packed. The crowd spilt out onto the foyer area as Jack, Suzette, and Phil took their seats at a table on the stage. Jack then moved to a microphone at center-stage and delivered a strong emotional speech about the difficulties facing Cranton. He pointed to the lack of good governance and how the situation would be remedied by voting for his team. Then Suzette and Phil provided their views about the type of actions that needed to be taken to revitalize the city.

At the end of the presentations the team of three, holding hands, walked to the front of the stage. They raised their arms in a salute to the crowd, which rose as one with a deafening ovation. Salina, who had been seated in the front row, was overcome with pride at the response that her husband and his team received. As he and Salina held hands and made their way through the crowd they were swamped with enthusiastic congratulations, both from those that they knew, and others that they were meeting for the first time.

After about half an hour the crowd began to disperse. Jack left Salina and Sam talking to a group of people that included Terry, his personal security guard, and entered a nearby bathroom. He was followed soon after by a burly man wearing dark glasses who entered a cubicle next to him. Then, while Jack was washing his hands, the man walked quickly up behind him, struck him a fierce blow to the ribs, threw him against a large mirror that came crashing to the floor and then hit him to the side of the head. Suddenly, a man entered the bathroom and confronted the assailant who pushed him aside and fled into the foyer followed by the man yelling for people to stop him. The heavily built thug was no match for the athletic Terry who launched a perfect flying tackle and brought him to the ground. Police were quickly on the scene and took the thug into custody.

Salina and Sam rushed into the bathroom to assist Jack who had struggled to his feet, insisting that he was OK. Salina was not so sure about that and asked Sam to call an ambulance to take him to hospital for a general check-over and images of his ribs and jaw.

The images revealed that he had two fractured ribs, plus he needed some stitches in a gash on his cheek that had been caused by a large ring that the thug had been wearing. Under questioning at the Cranton police station, the thug refused to reveal why he had attacked Jack and whether others were involved in planning the incident. He was charged with assault causing grievous bodily harm and detained on remand to await trial.

That evening, back at Gratton Grange, Salina received an anonymous phone call telling her that unless Jack withdrew from the mayoral campaign, she could expect further encouragement for him to do so. Following a discussion with Sam and Terry, it was agreed to increase security but not to tell Jack about the threat, as it was clear that he was absolutely committed to leading his team to victory in the election.

The next morning when Salina arrived at the hospital to take Jack home to Gratton Grange, he was sitting in the reception area waiting for her to arrive, endeavoring to project an impression that he was a bundle of energy.

"I have missed you darling. I'm feeling really good and can't wait to get back into the battle."

"You can't fool me Jack, I just saw you cough. You are obviously in a lot of pain with those damaged ribs, you need to get some rest and take it easy."

"Thanks for your concern, but the elections are next weekend and I need to be upright to lead my team to victory. I might even have the stitches out by then."

"I spoke to the doctor on the phone this morning and that's not what he told me."

"Maybe not, but I am the best one to know how I am feeling and what I believe I am capable of."

"I can imagine what your response would have been as a surgeon when dealing with one of your own patients. You would have told them in quite clear terms what was required for an effective recovery. Oh well, come with me. Disregarding good medical advice to the contrary, we will get on with what you are determined to do to save the city of Cranton."

Under the headline **Mayoral Candidate Bashed at Rally** the Chronicle ran a full front page reporting the attack at the town hall together with photos of the assailant being arrested by police and Jack being placed in an ambulance. Further editions of the paper carried several pages of letters to the editor deploring the incident and praising Jack for his courage in running for mayor. There was also considerable coverage on radio and television. It was a high price to pay for extensive publicity, but the attack had resulted in a huge uprising of support for Jack within the Cranton community.

On polling day Cambolli arrived early to cast his vote and talk to a few of his supporters who were distributing how-to-vote cards on his behalf at the town hall. Jack, Salina, Sam, and Joey had already arrived and planned to stay until the polls closed later in the day. Terry was also there with a reinforced contingent of security people, and there was a strong police presence.

Jack had only met Cambolli once before and was relieved that he did not attempt to come across and extend his hand, which would have been normal practice. Cambolli simply glanced in Jack's direction and nodded, as he and his entourage left after about half an hour.

That evening the Gratton Grange Estate restaurant was packed with invited family, friends, and close supporters of the Lansell team. There was also a significant police presence as well as Jack's personal security led by Terry. Crews from TV stations in Cranton, Baton Rouge and New Orleans had set up camp on the lawns and provided continuous coverage and commentary as the votes were counted under strict surveillance at the town hall. The election campaign for mayor had generated enormous interest throughout Louisiana and beyond.

Results did not take long to start coming through on television and radio, and a strong trend soon developed in favor of Jack and his team. By around 10.00 PM it was clear that Jack had been elected Mayor of Cranton with more than 80 percent of residents voting for him in an absolute election landslide. Overjoyed at the result, Jack hugged Salina and his team members. In front of the TV cameras, he said what an honor it was to be elected to such an important position at this challenging time in Cranton's history.

The next morning, he met with the doctor who had treated him at the hospital. Stitches in his cheek were removed and he was advised that his fractured ribs would take time to fully mend.

"You should avoid lifting heavy objects. The pain will gradually diminish. I would like to see your use of analgesics cease as soon as possible," the doctor said.

"OK Doc. Thanks for all your help, which is much appreciated."

"My pleasure Jack. I know that you have a busy and challenging schedule coming up, but just remember to try and take it easy for the next few weeks."

"Yep, thanks again Doc."

"I'm not convinced that my advice will be followed, but all the best and congratulations on being elected mayor. We sure need some new blood and an ethical leader to take us forward in this city."

CHAPTER 42

S traight after the meeting with the doctor Jack headed to the town hall for a meeting with the city manager, Kelvin Knox. This was a critical meeting with a man who he did not know well. He had put a lot of thought into how to handle the meeting and the form that it should take. In his position as city manager, Kelvin had extensive contact with Cambolli as mayor. In view of what Jack had learnt about Cambolli, some important questions needed to be answered about the nature of that relationship. However, he would need to keep an open mind until an investigation could be concluded into the finances and operations of City Hall.

At the meeting Jack asked Kelvin to provide several key documents including:

- Current operating and capital budgets
- Information on major programs and services
- An organization chart with key names and phone numbers
- Council rules and meeting procedures
- Meeting minutes for the last twelve months
- A comprehensive financial report

At the mention of the last item, Jack noticed a sudden tenseness come over Kelvin. His earlier confidence was less apparent.

"Mayor, I can provide you with most of the documents you are seeking right now, but the financial report may take a couple of days."

"I would like it by the end of this week please, so that I can study it prior to next week's council meeting."

"I will ensure that happens."

"Thanks Kelvin. I would now like to meet each of your key staff. After the next meeting of council, I would like the opportunity to address the entire staff and answer any questions they may have."

"I am sure all the staff would be interested in hearing personally from you. Come, and I will introduce you to my divisional heads."

The following week, after being officially installed as mayor and familiarizing himself with meeting procedures, Jack chaired his first meeting of Cranton City Council. At the recent elections, all existing councilors had been voted out of office. They had been replaced by Jack's team of three plus two new independent councilors. Kelvin Knox as city manager would attend meetings but did not have the right to vote on motions.

Jack opened the meeting with some comments about the important tasks ahead for the new council and invited Kelvin to outline the meeting procedures and the main items on the agenda for consideration. Jack then spoke to the main item which called for an independent audit of City Hall finances and emphasized that this was essential to provide an accurate and firm foundation upon which to revitalize the city. After much discussion about the many issues that needed to be confronted, the proposal was unanimously agreed. A leading New Orleans accountancy firm was authorized to undertake the task.

A couple of days later, representatives from the firm entered City Hall and set up operations in an allocated area of the council chambers. Jack directed Kelvin in clear terms to ensure that every assistance was to be provided to the auditors and no relevant information was to be withheld.

The front page of the Chronicle carried a bold headline announcing that external accountants had been appointed to inspect City Hall finances. This was accompanied by a photo of Jack and Kelvin with the accounting team. Since the council elections, Cambolli had not been sighted around town, but the story on the front page of the Chronicle would no doubt have caused him some consternation. Certainly, it was now the talk of the town.

The audit took almost a month to complete but a preliminary report was provided in time for the next council meeting. Jack advised Kelvin that the forthcoming meeting of the council would be held in camera, that the agenda would be primarily about the interim report, and that in the circumstances he should not attend.

The report had been sent to all councilors prior to the meeting so they were fully informed about the disturbing revelations. Numerous accounting discrepancies were revealed including payment of invoices for work that never happened. There were examples of major project expenditure without going to tender, as well as withholding important information and bypassing council. After lengthy discussion, it was unanimously agreed that Kelvin should be stood down and that when available the final report should be referred to the District Attorney for consideration and possible prosecutions.

The following morning Jack called Kelvin to his office and behind closed doors a heated discussion took place.

"Kelvin, as chief executive you are responsible and must have had considerable knowledge of the actions that led to this mess."

"I guess so, but Cambolli and his team on the council controlled the council and I was forced to comply with their directions."

"But did you ever stand up to them about the lack of ethics and threaten to expose them?"

"Mayor, you do not know what it is like to work with a man like Cambolli. He is a very intimidating and forceful person. He can be quite threatening."

"I understand that, but it was your duty not to bend to his wishes and to advise the appropriate authorities of the situation. I have spoken to the leader of the audit team about its preliminary report which strongly suggests that you colluded with Cambolli. I advise you that at last night's council meeting it was determined that you be stood down from your position as city manager. Security will escort you to your office, wait while you pack your personal belongings, and then escort you from the building."

Jack then phoned the Cranton District Attorney, Craig Farrow, and outlined what had occurred at the previous night's council meeting, including the decision to stand Kelvin down. He was not surprised when Farrow said he was already aware of the situation. It was agreed that Jack would join a meeting scheduled for the following day in Craig's office with Nathan Schilling from the Drug Enforcement Agency in Washington DC.

For Jack, this was a clear indication that the problems that the council was dealing with at City Hall were about to become part of a much wider investigation involving Cambolli.

CHAPTER 43

A s he entered Farrow's office for the meeting, Jack was reflecting on his recent retirement as a surgeon and how he had become embroiled in such an intricate situation which potentially involved far-reaching criminal activity. But it was not a time for reflecting, so he drew a deep breath and strode confidently forward with almost an air of exhilaration.

Craig Farrow greeted him warmly and introduced Nathan Schilling who explained that the DEA had been conducting an undercover investigation of Cambolli for some time. It was believed that he was the leader of a drug production and distribution racket out of his Cranton farming property.

"We know for sure that he is growing and distributing Cannabis at the property, and we suspect that other drugs are also being produced. But right now, we do not have any strong evidence of that," Nathan said.

"Craig has just briefed me on the information that you have provided about the issues surrounding Cambolli during his term as mayor of Cranton. He also told me that following a special council meeting you have taken action to stand down the city manager. Just prior to your arrival we have been discussing the possibility of undertaking joint action against Cambolli in relation to both drugs and his conduct as mayor."

Abruptly Craig, with a slightly raised voice and a look of determination, made a statement that startled Jack.

"We are considering a joint raid on the Cambolli property. It would involve DEA officers as well as selected local police. But first we would need to stand down the chief of police. We have been looking into his links with Cambolli. It is all starting to add up as to how Cambolli could conduct such an operation for so long without any supposed knowledge or action by the police."

"If you are going to stand down the chief of police, I think that it would need to happen concurrently with the raid on Cambolli. Otherwise, a warning would be conveyed that he could also be in trouble. Also, who would act in the chief's position?" asked Jack.

"Our view is that Marlon Doran is the man. He has been providing information to us and we recently spoke to him about identifying four trusted men should the need arise. What is your view?"

The officer suggested was the same man that Barry Blake at the Chronicle had told Jack was his informant about Cambolli's connection with the chief of police, Mick Marshall. An African American, and currently superintendent of traffic operations, Marlon was an outstanding experienced senior officer who had earlier been moved sideways from head of the crime squad by Marshall.

"I agree," said Jack without hesitation, and offered no further comment about that aspect of the plan.

"Good, we now need to move quickly on this to minimize the possibility of leaks occurring," replied Nathan. "My team of eight experienced special operations officers is primed to go. I will give them a final briefing later today when I get back to Washington. I propose that we carry out the joint operation at dawn the day after tomorrow. My team and I will fly in from Washington tomorrow and stay overnight in a property that we have already rented on the edge of the city, about one mile from the target property. Marlon and the four police officers provided by him for the operation will also stay at that property tomorrow night. They will receive a final briefing about their role which will include responsibility for transporting the team to the Cambolli property."

That evening over dinner, Jack outlined the day's events to Salina who had trouble believing what she was hearing.

"Who would ever have thought that things would come to this in the once lovely and relatively quiet city of Cranton. It sounds more like something that would happen in some crime thriller series on television."

"Well darling, be prepared, because I strongly suspect that the city and you and I are about to be featured on national television."

"I haven't bought a new dress for a while so maybe this is as good an opportunity as any," she said, only half joking.

"You had better hurry and go shopping tomorrow because events are moving very fast."

CHAPTER 44

The next night Nathan moved with his men into the rented property under the cloak of darkness with Marlon and his men in three unmarked police SUV vehicles and a van. A detailed briefing was provided by Nathan about the action to be commenced at dawn when Marlon and his men would transport Nathan and his team to Cambolli's property. Concurrently, Craig Farrow would move to have Mick Marshall brought in for questioning and charged in relation to colluding with Cambolli.

At the first hint of dawn breaking, the police vehicles sped up Cambolli's driveway to his house beside a large barn-like outbuilding. Shielded by the vehicles, Nathan and Marlon took up a position near the front of the house and through a loud hailer Nathan advised Cambolli and his men that they were surrounded.

"I have a warrant to search the premises for illicit drugs. You and your men are ordered to come forward with hands in the air. You are also advised that Mick Marshall is right now being questioned about collusion with you in relation to drug production and distribution."

Soon after, three men appeared from the barn and were quickly cuffed and locked in the police van. Another came out from the house and said that Cambolli refused to come forward. He said he was instructed by Cambolli to convey that he was an innocent man who had arrived from Italy several years ago with very little. He believed that he had contributed a lot to the local community and was now being persecuted for his efforts by the new mayor.

Over the loud hailer, Nathan told him it was in his best interests to come forward, otherwise they would forcibly enter his house and bring him out. Soon after a small-arms shot was heard from within the house and Nathan ordered his men to enter. They found Cambolli slumped in an armchair in the lounge with his head on his chest and a gunshot wound to his temple.

Marlon immediately radioed for an ambulance and rang Craig Farrow to advise him of what had happened. By this time officers had entered the barn and found a range of sophisticated drug-making equipment and chemicals. They were amazed at the scale of the operation that also included large racks for drying harvested cannabis crops.

The sound of an ambulance siren greeted residents in the early morning as it raced through the city. It was not long before media representatives including Barry Blake arrived on the scene followed by Jack who had been contacted by Nathan. A doctor from the Cranton hospital also arrived to examine Cambolli and soon after pronounced him dead. By now many questions were being fired at Nathan and Jack by the media as to the reasons for the raid which had resulted in several arrests and the death of the former mayor. After consulting Nathan, Jack spoke briefly and advised that a full media briefing would be held at midday at the town hall.

As Cambolli's body, covered by a sheet, was wheeled on a trolley from his house and placed in the ambulance, Jack's thoughts ran to the type of person that he turned out to be. Here was a man who had arrived in Cranton with next to nothing, became quite a successful legitimate businessman, and even mayor of the city. How could he then turn to corporate crime and, worst of all, become involved in an illicit drug racket? He figured that selfishness and greed must have had a lot to do with the path that his life took, and which led to his eventual demise.

Jack's office phone was now running hot with media enquiries, not only from within Louisiana, but also from several other states around the US. Jack and the council's communications manager had drafted a media release for general distribution immediately after the media briefing. A special media briefing room had been setup at the town hall and Jack, Nathan Schilling, Craig Farrow, and Marlon Doran as acting chief of police, would front the eager media throng. Salina would also be present and take a seat at the back of the briefing room.

The two trials that followed in New Orleans attracted enormous media attention. Mick pleaded guilty and was sentenced to a substantial jail term due to the position of trust that he held as a senior public servant. He received some leniency due to his guilty plea.

Kelvin pleaded not guilty on the basis that he was harassed and threatened by Cambolli as mayor and by his associates on the municipal council. The judge felt that he had some possibility of rehabilitation and brought down a reduced jail sentence.

It was a hot day as Jack drove back to Gratton Grange after witnessing the sentencing of Kelvin. Salina sat next to him wearing a light summer dress which she had pulled up above her knees.

"Nice knees Salina, and a pretty dress."

"Thank you, mayor. Would you like to know what's underneath?"

"A pair of knickers I presume."

"Would you like to see?"

Without waiting for a response, she drew her dress up to her waste as Jack squinted across to get a view, trying to keep one eye on the road ahead.

"Did you actually sit in the court next to me like that?"

"No, as it was so hot, I took my knickers off in the bathroom before we left the court."

"Very commendable of you to think ahead about being comfortable for the drive home."

"Why are we now going up this little side road?"

"Because I need to have a closer investigation to establish the real reason for your beguiling lack of modesty. This is a secluded place to do that, your honor."

"So, you have now gone from being mayor to chief investigator?"

"Yes, and I am very excited about the prospects of this new role."

CHAPTER 45

O ver dinner at home Belinda noticed that Sam was unusually quiet. She asked if something was wrong.

"No, nothing is wrong. I am a happy man. It's just that since turning 65 I have been thinking that maybe it's time for me to retire as general manager at Gratton Grange."

"Has this thinking been influenced by Jack's recent retirement as a surgeon and his reincarnation as Cranton mayor?"

"That is probably what started me thinking about the future. You and I have worked hard and led an immensely rewarding life here. Maybe it is now time for us to 'smell the roses', as they say. We could buy a nice home in New Orleans and travel to the many parts of this country we have never seen. Maybe we could also do some overseas travel, especially in Europe. It would be great if somehow we could also maintain an involvement at Gratton Grange."

"I like your ideas very much. We should turn them into action. Why don't we arrange a meeting soon with Jack and Salina?" suggested Belinda.

The meeting was held over lunch at a quiet corner table in the Gratton Grange Estate restaurant. Jack told Sam that he was not surprised at his plan to retire.

"You and Belinda have made an enormous contribution to the success of Gratton Grange. Salina and I fully understand your decision. Sam, we are also keen to retain your involvement with the company in some way. Would you agree to an arrangement whereby you remain as a board member as well as take up a part-time position as consultant to whoever is the new general manager at Gratton Grange?"

Sam looked at Belinda, who nodded enthusiastically.

"OK, we will have a new employment contract drawn up," said Jack. "Sam, this is a great moment in our relationship that started when we first met at that bar in New Orleans. We have both come a long way since then. How wonderful that we can sit here many years later as close friends and again plan our way ahead. We have had an enormous impact on each other's lives, especially you on my life by introducing me to this wonderful lady," Jack said, putting his arm around Salina.

He had difficulty controlling his emotions at such a watershed moment. "I guess we will now have to think about who will replace you as general manager."

"Can I suggest that you will not have to look very far," Sam said. "Marcus would be perfect for the job. He has a lot of energy, a good understanding of the overall operations here, and is well settled in a strong relationship with Naomi. Due to his university training and current employment as an agricultural scientist he will also bring a lot of relevant up-to-date knowledge to the role. Marcus and Joey get along well and would form a good team. Belinda and I plan to purchase a home in New Orleans, so maybe Marcus and Naomi could move into Cooper's former house where we currently live."

"I agree. Marcus would be an excellent choice," said an enthusiastic Salina. "This arrangement could also have the added benefit of enabling Naomi to become involved in Gratton Grange operations. She has shown a lot of interest in the apiary so perhaps she could take over management of Gratton Grange Honey. That would enable me to concentrate more on further developing the vineyard business."

"I must admit that it crossed my mind recently about who might one day take over from Sam," said Jack. "It seems that we are all in agreement. I will contact Marcus today and sound him out."

Marcus and Naomi were invited for dinner at the manor house.

"Well, what do you think about our proposal," asked Jack, looking searchingly at Marcus and then Naomi for a reaction.

"This is the culmination of a dream that I had when I first visited Gratton Grange while still at school in New York," responded Marcus. "I am so pleased that you believe in my ability to take over from such an outstanding and valued manager as Sam. It is good that he will be available to provide some guidance and advice, especially in the early stages of my new role. I will do my best to fulfill your expectations. Naomi, will you join me at Gratton Grange? I know that you love your job at the yacht club, but this is a great opportunity for us."

"I can't wait to start," said an excited Naomi. The bees and I get along well. I am fascinated by the benefits they bring to our world and the beautiful honey they produce. Also, I will be able to see and ride Chiquita more often. Thank you so much. I am honored by your offer. My father is not going to believe that I am now the manager of a honey business. I am sure he will be extremely proud."

Soon after Sam and Belinda moved into their newly purchased terrace house in New Orleans, and moved out of their house at Gratton Grange, Naomi and Salina began a refurbishment of the property. New drapes were ordered, the kitchen was updated, and the rooms were repainted in Naomi's favorite colors, including orange ochre in the dining room.

"Why don't we have a timber deck and pergola constructed across the front of the house?" suggested Salina. "It could have a canopy of grape vines from root stock that I can supply from the vineyard. That would be great for entertaining guests on a balmy evening, of which there are many in Louisiana as you would have noticed."

"Yes, and Marcus and I could buy a barbeque for the deck to sizzle steaks and sausages, just like we did in Darwin. This is an amazing new adventure. Sometimes I have difficulty believing I am even part of it."

"Naomi, talking about the vineyard, I think it would be good for you to gradually gain some experience in operating a vineyard so that you can assist me. You could take over sometimes when I am on holiday. I am a great believer in multi-skilling where possible in Gratton Grange operations. It would also help if you could do a part-time course in viticulture like I once did."

"Count me in Salina. I too am a great believer in multi-skilling."

CHAPTER 46

After moving from Baton Rouge into the condominium at Cranton owned by Rick and Lorie, Louise and Brendon relaxed happily on the upstairs balcony watching the traffic pass by on the Mississippi River. They discussed progress in undertaking the establishment of Cranton Construction and timeframes for the operational way ahead.

It was a challenging but exciting time. A temporary office had been set up for the new company in an old building near the city center. Following approval of plans by the local authorities, work had commenced to prepare the land now owned by the company on the edge of the city for a new housing estate. Wasting no time, they were also working closely with Rick and architects on the design of a new commercial and shopping precinct in the center of the city. When completed, Cranton Construction would move into offices in the new stylish development. An associated business, Cranton Recycling, would be established in the city's existing industrial area.

"Louise, our responsibilities seem to be naturally evolving with you looking after the administrative side, and me handling construction projects in the field," observed Brendon. "This seems to be working out quite well. As joint managing director are you happy for this type of arrangement to continue?"

"You are reading my mind. I am more than happy for us to continue like that. I think such an arrangement suits our individual personalities and talents. I can't imagine an athletic person such as yourself being couped up in an office for long," she said with a laugh. "On the other hand, I relate well to working with figures, monitoring project performance, studying industry trends, and ensuring proper governance."

He picked her up, swung her around in the air, kissed her, and said: "You and I are becoming a great team, my beautiful Louise. I am so glad you finally relented when I persistently tried to chat you up at university. How quickly time passes. Look at the progress we are now making with our lives."

Following approval of plans to develop a new city square on land owned by the city, several dilapidated buildings were demolished and much of the materials were transported to Cranton Recycling. Work then commenced to construct a spacious modern plaza to house a wide range of shops and a large supermarket. On the opposite side of the square, that would be grassed and include paved sections and extensive plantings, a three-story office block with below-ground parking began to take shape. A range of cafes, a couple of high-end French and Italian restaurants, and a Spanish tapas bar, would spring up on the ground floor of a multi-story residential tower on another side of the square.

During the planning stage, Salina had attended a meeting with Rick, Louise, and Brendon where it was agreed that provision for an art gallery, theatres, and a public library would be incorporated into the city center concept. She was particularly keen that the art gallery provide an ongoing showcase to exhibit the work of artists from across Louisiana, as well as encourage exhibitions of the works of famous painters from around the world.

"Maybe we could even host an exhibition of famous French Impressionists, including my favorite, Manet. Who knows, once we get set up, the sky's the limit," she said with great enthusiasm.

The people of Cranton had never seen such activity in their city. Building skeletons suddenly appeared surrounded with scaffolding, large concrete mixer trucks came and went, and huge cranes lifted building materials skywards at the blast of a whistle. The pace was almost frenetic. Working in conjunction with Ken, the site manager, Brendon was in his element ensuring that all materials and trades arrived on time, in the right location, and at the agreed price. He was also responsible for quality control as work progressed, including external cladding, the enormous windows, and the quality of paint work.

Ken ensured that various tradespeople, including carpenters, plumbers, and electricians, moved quickly around the site according to a schedule of requirements he had prepared. Louise, Brendon, and Ken met at the close of work each day to review progress and ensure that there were no problems, especially cost blowouts against contracts and budgets.

The number of local tradespeople engaged on the huge project had to be boosted by bringing in others from out of town. People who had been unemployed suddenly had jobs. The whole local economy benefited enormously from the sudden increase in activity, including shopkeepers, suppliers of materials, and local providers of accommodation.

Salina took a personal interest in the design and development of the expansive public space of the city square. She requested that a large water feature including a fountain be installed at the center of the square. Around the entire perlmeter of the circular water feature specially designed continuous timber seating would be installed. Trees were planted, and many large planter boxes filled with multi-colored flowers were installed throughout the square.

She wanted the whole area to be a place of fun, relaxation, and culture, as well as a shopping and commerce center.

"All people, regardless of color, race, religion or politics will be welcome. We must strive to ensure that this happens. The benefits could be enormous, both economically and socially. This can be just the start of a much bigger plan to revitalize Cranton," she said in an interview with the Chronicle.

For the grand opening of the glittering new city center a large stage was erected and a vibrant happy carnival atmosphere was created. There were clowns on stilts, jugglers, and buskers as well as balloons, popcorn, and face painting for the kids. In the pond around the fountain kids jumped in and out, squealing as they splashed water over each other.

The city square was soon packed with locals and many people from out of town. From the stage Jack, as Cranton mayor, welcomed the crowd and said what a momentous occasion the event was in the history of the city. He paid tribute to all who had been involved in bringing such a huge visionary project to fruition, especially Rick Mangan, his daughter Louise, and her partner Brendon.

Salina, Lorie, Louise, Nora, and Naomi, as well as Eloise, who was down from New York for the event, were talking near the stage when Louise asked her mother Lorie where Rick was.

"He is up there with his buddies on the third floor of that building over there, trying to keep a low profile," she said, pointing to a crowded balcony. "He has left it to Jack to do all the talking to the people of Cranton. That's the way he operates. For him the job is done, with no big fanfare, just a feeling of subdued pride, and a quiet beer with his pals. That's my Rick – it's one of the reasons I love him so much. Look, he's not even at the front of that big balcony but sitting right at the back. Rick is so competent, but so low profile, God love him."

Naomi commented on how nice it was that Lorie and Rick obviously had such a strong relationship.

"We do, but Rick is not the easiest man to get to know," responded Lorie. "In many ways he is a humble man devoid of any pretentions. At times he can be quite confronting, but underneath there is a heart of gold. I would trust him with my life."

Louise looked at her mother, surprised at her unexpected comments. She took her hand and said: "I love him too mother, and I must say, Brendon certainly holds him in high regard."

Brendon and Marcus were also with the group up on the balcony, as well as Rick's best friend Andy who owned a hotel in Baton Rouge, and Brendon's father Gerard. Alex, who had arrived a few days earlier from Darwin, was there after enjoying a sail on Lake Pontchartrain the previous day with Gerard, Brendon, and Marcus.

"I can see my father Alex up there drinking a beer," said Naomi. "He has taken a liking to the local brews, but then I must say he enjoys almost any beer," she added with a laugh.

The group on the balcony were drinking complimentary beer supplied by Andy's hotel.

"Hey Rick, how come you are not down there saying a few words to the crowd about your amazing concept which has now come to fruition in Cranton," enquired Andy.

"My job is over, Jack is handling all that commentary stuff," was the short response from Rick.

"So, do you have any plans for your next project?"

"Lorie believes it's time for a holiday, so at my suggestion, after listening to the great time that Brendon and Marcus had in Darwin, we have booked to go there. The trip will include a tour of a place south of Darwin where we will go on a boat cruise and see huge crocodiles, water buffalo and a great variety of birdlife. We can also try some bush tucker for dinner one night."

"The place you are talking about southeast of Darwin is Kakadu National Park, which will be an unforgettable experience. Does Lorie also plan to join you in sampling bush tucker? For some it can be a challenging experience," said Brendon.

"Lorie said she will think about that when we get there, but she did suggest she might just settle for barramundi cooked on the coals that you told her about."

The discussion on the balcony was broken by a loud cheer that went up as Jack introduced the recently formed local rock band *Moovin & Groovin*. Balloons floated through the air and streamers descended from upstairs balconies around the square as people began singing and dancing to the beat of the band.

And then the well-known *Big Easy Band* from New Orleans took the stage. The exuberant mood of the crowd settled slightly. There was a feeling of expectation in the air. A drum roll introduced a stirring jazz trumpet solo before the full band launched into the soundtrack of *Summertime*. The crowd yelled for Salina. Suddenly, the band stopped playing.

"You have got to get up there, especially on an occasion like this," said an excited Eloise, grabbing her mother's hand. "The people want you."

"But I have not performed for a long time now. I'm not sure I can do it."

"You know the band. You are a professional. Performing is in your blood. You will be fine."

As she walked to the microphone the applause was deafening. She sang *Summertime* almost like it had been composed for her. As she moved to leave the stage the crowd wanted more. She finished with a beautiful rendition of *Blue Skies,* which she had last sung in Paris while on her honeymoon many years before.

Naomi was amazed at the reception that Salina received from the crowd. Turning to Eloise she said: "What a woman. Your mother is an absolute star. I am honored to know and work with her, and especially to have her as a friend."

Around sunset, the rock band came back on stage to take the Cranton festivities into the night.

As she left with Jack, Salina's thoughts turned to relief at how well the Cranton rejuvenation strategy was evolving and how proud she was of Jack's role. She had learnt a lot about her own character including the resilience that she had managed to display. But most of all, she was impressed by Jack's strength in carrying through with his determination to take on the position of mayor against frightening opposition. 'And now look at the result', she thought. Walking to his SUV, she squeezed his hand and got a big smile in return – there was no need for words.

CHAPTER 47

A fter leaving her job at the yacht club Naomi emersed herself enthusiastically into managing the apiary and commenced the development of export markets for Gratton Grange Honey. Following Salina's suggestion, she also undertook a part-time course in viticulture and began assisting her in operation of the vineyard.

At the start of summer, Marcus spoke to Brendon about making plans to once again visit Darwin for the yachting regatta.

"Buddy, I would love to go but Louise and I are just too busy with development of the new housing estate in Cranton right now. If you go, would you please give my regards to Alex and the others at the yacht club," requested Brendon.

Marcus had already talked to Naomi about returning to Darwin for a few days and she was keen to see her father again. There was also another good reason for a trip to Darwin – over a quiet dinner at Sirico's, Naomi had accepted Marcus's proposal of marriage.

The happy couple told the exciting news to Jack and Salina. It was agreed that Joey would fill in for Marcus during their brief absence in Darwin and Salina would look after the Gratton Grange Honey business.

On the plane on the way to Australia, Marcus commented to Naomi that they should look for an engagement ring in Darwin.

"Have you thought about the type of ring that you would like."

"Yes, I have. Let me show you?"

On the back of a Qantas menu, she sketched the ring that she had been dreaming about.

"I do not want a traditional diamond ring. Darwin is the home of world famous Paspaley South Sea Pearls. My ring will have a large solitary Paspaley pearl mounted prominently in a little gold cup on a plain rose gold band – like this," she said, completing the sketch. "What do you think of my idea?"

"It sounds beautiful and will always provide an important link for you, back to your city of birth. I think it's a wonderful idea."

Once again, they stayed at Alex's home in Callum Bay where their romance had really ignited on the boat after her 21st birthday celebrations. That night really marked the point of no return in their relationship. They had become a committed loving couple.

At a quiet moment on the balcony of the yacht club Marcus asked Alex for permission to marry his daughter.

"I was getting a little worried after you took her to the other side of the world. But now you have redeemed yourself by proposing to her, and even asking for my permission. I am most impressed," Alex said with a cheeky grin.

The next morning, the happy couple raced into central Darwin to visit Naomi's favorite jeweler. She presented him with the sketch she had prepared of the type of ring she wanted.

"Hi James, I do not want a traditional diamond ring. This one must have a superb large solitaire Paspaley pearl that sits high on a plain rose gold band. It should have no embellishments. For this ring, less is more. Can you do this quickly for me?"

"This is an unusual but most interesting design. I am impressed. We should be able to deliver within the next few days," he said, taking a sizing of her finger.

Three days later they collected the ring which came in an attractive orange ochre-colored box, much to Naomi's delight. The ring was just as beautiful as she imagined and fitted perfectly.

James presented her with a bunch of red roses to mark the occasion.

"Naomi, these are to wish you and Marcus a wonderful happy life together. Not only are you a dear friend, you are also an excellent designer."

That afternoon they showed the ring to Alex.

"That is a magnificent, understated ring. It has a great presence with its solitaire local pearl and plain band. Who designed it?"

Marcus handed the Qantas menu to Alex and pointed to Naomi, who blushed and pulled her hat down over her face.

"Congratulations, I am so pleased for you both," he said, producing a bottle of sparkling Australian Chandon Brut and three glasses. They then headed to a restaurant at the Callum Bay marina to celebrate.

Over lunch at the marina the following day, Naomi asked Alex how Sharon, who had replaced her in his business, was going.

"Although she had virtually no experience in boating supplies and boat brokerage, she is a member of the yacht club and a good sailor with many contacts in the world of sailing and boating in general. As you know, I met her not long after you went to live in the US and the relationship has developed from friendship to something closer than that."

"Really? Tell us more." said Naomi, peering with a rather searching, inquisitive look across the table at Alex. "How capable is she?"

Immediately, Naomi wished she had not asked that. 'I must sound like I may have an issue with Sharon entering my father's life, or maybe that I am too protective. How silly of me she thought.'

Marcus recognized and understood how difficult it must be sometimes for Naomi to deal with conflicting considerations relating to her relocation from her homeland to another country so far away. Various feelings could easily become confusing, especially when talking about a woman who had taken her place in the business and who she had never met. He was quick to intervene to defuse the situation, boost Naomi's confidence, and help her relax.

"Alex, it must have been difficult initially for you to cover Naomi's role in the business, but it sounds like Sharon is now growing into the job quite nicely. I must say, the work that Naomi is doing at Gratton Grange is producing excellent results. Not only is she running Gratton Grange Honey almost single handedly, but she is taking a lot of the pressure off Salina in developing the vineyard. Looks like overall we have a win-win situation, here and in Louisiana. Hey Alex, is that your cabin cruiser tying up at the wharf?"

"Yes, I have not been using it much lately, so hired it out for a few hours. Those people will leave it here and we will motor it back to my jetty instead of walking back."

The next day Naomi drove Alex and Marcus to the yacht club where they would sleep aboard *Sunburst* and compete in the regatta over the weekend. She then drove to the cattle station where she received a warm welcome from Larry and checked into a cabin for two nights. In return for accommodation, she would assist with jobs around the homestead and take the opportunity to ride Lady after being assured in advance that the horse would be available.

As Naomi walked to the paddock Lady came galloping up to the fence, threw her head in the air and, with a type of prancing movement, took the apple that Naomi offered. It was a sign that their unusual friendship had been renewed.

Shortly before Marcus and Naomi were scheduled to fly back to New Orleans, they tried to talk Alex into going with them for another holiday in Louisiana.

"I would love to do that, but I just don't have enough time to make the necessary business arrangements here to cover my absence," he said. "Sharon now has a good understanding of how the business operates, but I would need enough time to brief her on a couple of likely yacht sales that look like coming off soon.

"We understand," said Marcus. "Let's agree that you will come over before the end of our summer. You can stay at Gratton Grange, catch up with Jack, go sailing with Brendon and me again, enjoy the vibrant atmosphere of the New Orleans French Quarter, and this time listen to some great jazz on a Mississippi paddle steamer. How about that for another holiday?"

"Fantastic. I will start preparations and book a flight in the next few days."

Soon after arriving home Marcus and Naomi had lunch with Brendon and Louise at the new French restaurant in Cranton city square.

"Congratulations Naomi. I just love that ring," said Louise. "Is it true that you designed it."

Lacking an immediate response from Naomi, Marcus quickly said: "Yes, it is. She sketched it during the flight to Darwin on the back of a Qantas menu."

"How amazing. What a great story. We too have some news – Brendon and I are also engaged after he plucked up the courage to ask my father's permission. We collect the ring tomorrow. I must admit that I did not design it, but I did give clear instructions as to what I wanted. It will feature a solitaire sapphire on a plain white gold band."

"Gosh." said Naomi. "That sounds beautiful. Congratulations to you both. What great news. How good is it that we four are all here right now, celebrating together?"

"Yes, but of course it would not have happened without my bravery in approaching Rick about my wish to marry his daughter," laughed Brendon, putting his arm around Louise. "Waiter, would you please bring a bottle of Veuve Clicquot Brut and four glasses."

CHAPTER 48

After some years in New York studying music at the conservatory, Eloise was preparing for assessment before graduating. In her final year she had specialized in the violin and had a strong interest in chamber jazz.

Prior to arriving in New York, Jack had arranged for her to move into the apartment on Long Island that he still owned. Eloise was happy there, having joined the local tennis club and being close to her grandparents who had moved into a nearby retirement village. Through the week, from Monday to Thursday, she shared an apartment near the conservatory with two girlfriends who were also students. Early on most Fridays, she would drive to Long Island and then return to Manhattan on Monday morning.

Lindsay, her boyfriend of just a few months, wanted her to reside in Manhattan full-time, but she refused, preferring to spend weekends in the more relaxed atmosphere of Long Island.

"You don't understand," she told him. "I have the best of both worlds. There is the exciting hustle and bustle of New York, and not far away is the lovely serenity of Long Island. I also have the benefit of earning some money at a café by waitressing there at weekends."

Following her brief stay down south for the Cranton festivities, Eloise met Lindsay for coffee on Fifth Avenue. Working for an insurance brokerage, he was an ambitious highly opinionated young man. Some might say a bit of a snob and social climber.

"Why are you looking at me like that?" she asked.

"Like what?"

"Like you don't approve of what you see."

"Is that a new dress?"

"Yes. I get the impression that you don't like it."

"It's OK but not very fashionable. You tend to dress very conservatively sometimes my dear."

"For your information mister know-all, it comes from a recently released collection of stylish new fashions by leading designers. No doubt you would like it to be shorter with a plunging neckline, but I prefer this classy, more sophisticated look. And please do not patronize me by calling me 'your dear', especially when you have just insulted me."

"I'm sorry, I did not mean to do that. When is your graduation ceremony?" he asked, gulping down some coffee and trying to change the subject.

"Next week. I guess you expect to be invited," she quipped.

"Am I invited?"

"I guess so."

With that, she rose, turned her back, and walked to a nearby supermarket to shop for dinner ingredients before heading to the apartment that she shared.

Jack and Salina, together with Marcus and Naomi, flew to New York for Eloise's graduation. As she came forward in her graduate gown and mortarboard to receive her degree with honors, Salina shed a tear and observed how happy her daughter looked.

"Jack, it seems like just yesterday that I drove her into Cranton when she started school. She was jumping around and eager to make new friends. I am so proud of her."

"She is a talented young lady with a great understanding and appreciation of music, much of which I believe has been passed on from you," said Jack.

After the mid-morning presentations, a large crowd mingled in the hall, enjoying coffee, tea, assorted cookies, and muffins.

Eloise raced across and embraced Salina and Jack.

"What do you think of my new gear?" she asked, twirling around showing off her graduation gown.

"Absolutely wonderful," said an ecstatic Salina. "Sometime soon, maybe you could play the violin and I could sing. Wouldn't that be good?"

"We must make that happen," said an excited Eloise.

Lindsay, who had been talking with a group of people across the other side of the hall, suddenly appeared and was introduced to Eloise's family.

They chatted briefly before she took him aside and told him she was not impressed with how he had ignored her on such an important day by talking to others, and only now coming over.

"You are a very self-centered person, Lindsay. Our relationship, such as it was, has run its course. Goodbye and good luck."

With a sigh of relief, she returned to the company of her family.

"There is some great news that I must tell you. A few days ago, I was invited to join a chamber jazz ensemble. It is a well-known and highly regarded group in New York. I signed a contract last night and my first performance with the ensemble will be at the Plaza Hotel next month. Will you be able to come back for that? It would mean so much to me."

"What wonderful news. We will definitely be there," said Jack as Salina and Naomi hugged Eloise. "Why don't we go to The Plaza now for lunch. I will make a dinner booking for the night of your performance. This is a great moment. I am so pleased for you."

The next Saturday afternoon, as Eloise arrived at the tennis club on Long Island, she was approached by a tall suntanned man in his mid-twenties who she had met once before at the club.

"Eloise, would you like to partner me in mixed doubles?" asked Greg. "The partner that I had last weekend has moved to Boston with her work."

"OK, thanks for the invitation, but I do not have much experience in doubles."

"Don't worry. What with my serve and your great cross-court forehand, that I noticed last weekend, we could be quite competitive."

Later, after narrowly losing a friendly match, Eloise prepared to leave the club when Greg asked her if she would like to join him for dinner.

"That would be nice, but I am committed to do some waitressing tonight. Maybe next Saturday?"

"Great. What type of food do you like?"

"I grew up in New Orleans and have experienced a wide variety of cuisine. My favorite is French."

"I will make a booking at the French restaurant down the road and call for you at around 7.30 PM next Saturday. Here is my card. Please write down your address and phone number for me."

The following Saturday over dinner, Greg commented on how nice Eloise looked in her stylish layered crimson dress and dark hair down on her shoulders.

"You wear clothes with a sense of style and an air of confidence. I noticed that when I first saw you at the tennis club."

"Thank you, Greg. I do not have an extensive wardrobe, but the clothes that I have are stylish and good quality. I think that is important. It reflects one's personality and values. Have you always lived on Long Island?"

"Yes. My parents own a local plant nursery which no doubt helps to explain how I come to be in the landscaping business. The two businesses complement each other very nicely."

Eloise explained that her parents owned Gratton Grange, told him about the diverse business operations there, and how she came to divide her time between Manhattan and Long Island.

"I am about to enter an extremely exciting time in my life. My music career will be launched next month at the Plaza Hotel. Maybe you would like to join us there for the occasion?"

"Thank you. I would love to do that. Here's to the launch of Eloise Lansell into the chamber music world," he said enthusiastically as the waiter topped up their glasses.

CHAPTER 49

A large audience had gathered to hear the first performance of the jazz ensemble at The Plaza. Jack and Salina, Marcus and Naomi, were there together with Eloise's grandparents from Long Island, her grandmother from Montgomery, Sam and Belinda, and her new friend Greg.

The ensemble had been tuning instruments and adjusting arrangements for its performance. As people arrived, Louise walked down and greeted her family and friends. Greg gave her a kiss on the cheek and wished her well as she introduced him to Jack and Salina.

As they took their seats, Marcus explained to Naomi that jazz chamber music was a combination of jazz and classical music that delivered the great rhythms of jazz influenced by the structure of classical orchestration.

"I see it as an exciting merging of the music of south and north in this country," he said.

The jazz chamber ensemble consisted of piano, saxophone, clarinet, cello, acoustic guitar, and Eloise on violin.

Towards the end of the performance the ensemble leader came to the microphone and announced that a renowned jazz singer from New Orleans was in the audience. He invited Salina to come forward and join them for a couple of numbers.

An embarrassed Salina resisted until Eloise came over, took her hand, and walked with her to the microphone. Placing her violin under her chin, Eloise stood beside her mother and led her into a beautiful version of Cole Porter's *Night & Day* followed by Salina's own upbeat jazz version of *New York, New York* made famous by Liza Minnelli and Frank Sinatra. At the conclusion of the song Salina told the audience that she had always loved New York.

"This city has a special place in my heart, not least because it provided me with my wonderful husband Jack, who is sitting right over there. I find it hard to believe that I have been given this opportunity here tonight – two girls from The Big Easy performing in The Big Apple. It is an absolute delight to be at this famous hotel with my daughter Eloise beside me. Thank you dear for dragging me to the microphone."

There was sustained applause as mother and daughter bowered and Salina moved back to her seat.

At the end of the chamber ensemble performance the party of family and friends moved into the dining room for dinner. Greg took Eloise's hand which was intended to send a signal that they were now a couple.

Towards the end of dinner, while Greg visited the bathroom, Jack quietly commented to Eloise that he was a huge improvement on Lindsay.

"It is early days in our relationship, but I really like this guy. There is a lot in common. We both come from an outdoors background. He has shown a lot of interest in what you are doing at Gratton Grange. At some stage I would like to bring him down there to visit. Also, would you believe, he reckons if we keep practicing, we could be the next mixed doubles champions of the tennis club. How about that?" she said with a laugh.

Soon after returning from New York, Jack and Salina sat on the end of the jetty at Gratton Grange, legs dangling over, where many years before he had proposed to her. They looked out over the Mississippi River, reminiscing about their life together now that Marcus had taken over from Sam as plantation manager. Music from the Mississippi Princess as it passed travelled across the water, including the song *Summertime*.

"You know Jack, *Summertime* is my favorite song. Do you remember that I sang it on the night we met in Sirico's? That song always makes me feel quite emotional – Summertime in The Big Easy."

"How lucky we are to be able to sit here like this, so happy and with so much still to look forward to," said Jack. "Thank you for agreeing to marry me Mrs. Lansell. You are so beautiful, not only on the outside but especially with that wonderful soul that you have on the inside. I am such a lucky man."

She put her arm around him, saying softly: "And I am such a fortunate woman, Dr Lansell, my magnificent plantation man."

ACKNOWLEDGEMENTS

During the writing of *Plantation Man,* my debut novel, I received significant encouragement and valuable commentary from friend, editor, author, and fellow writer, John Power. Generous guidance that he provided included suggestions on controlling the pace and direction of the storyline development, appropriate use of narrative and dialogue, and the importance of revealing the detailed in-depth thought processes of characters. John emphasized to me that a central focus when writing a novel should be to 'show' rather than 'tell' the reader.

As the manuscript progressed, various views were also provided by close friends and family members. Retired accountant friend, Barrie Barton, was a regular contributor of mostly positive comments over numerous coffees at my home. Another friend, former corporate communications manager, Russell Nowell provided helpful suggestions about the structure of the storyline.

Helpful comments on parts of the manuscript were also provided by family members including my nephew John Ostermeyer, nephew Brad Ostermeyer and his wife Brooke, and my niece Dr Annette Ostermeyer and her husband Gareth.

Finally, I must acknowledge the expertise and commitment of Ian Bosler and staff at Intertype Publish and Print who were instrumental in bringing *Plantation Man* to life as a published book.

ABOUT THE AUTHOR

Hartley Henderson has worked on both sides of the media fence – as part of the media as a journalist, and at other times dealing with the media as a corporate communications manager.

For the past 20 years he has worked as a freelance writer for a wide range of industry-focused magazines. He has also written advertising copy, video film scripts, newsletters, and speeches for senior people within industry and government.

Hartley lives on the Mornington Peninsula in Victoria, Australia, and has travelled widely, especially in the USA.

www.ingramcontent.com/pod-product-compliance
Lightning Source LLC
Chambersburg PA
CBHW072353030726
47505CB00014B/1805